Petticoats and Pioneers

Malania E. Reynolds

 THREE SKILLET

One

The sound of a barking dog awoke Josiah Hadley from a sound sleep. He was halfway across the room, his gun in his hand, before he realized it wasn't Jack, his dog, who had caused the ruckus. He stumbled to the window of his hotel room and fingered a small slit in the side of the shade to look down onto the street.

"Damn," he muttered. A man was staggering drunkenly down the street, the dog snapping at his heels. "Doesn't the fool know it's the middle of the night?"

The circle of light from the street lamp on the pole showed him to be middle aged and portly. The man tossed a pebble at the dog and the small creature backed away, his tail between his legs. Rubbing his face the way Joe had seen drunken men do, the fool leaned on the pole a moment before staggering on down the road.

Joe put his pistol back in its holster, hanging on the bedpost. He reached for his shirt and yawned, muttering, "No sense in sleeping now. Might as well beat the world to my business. Somebody's got to come out ahead, and it might as well be me."

He wrapped the shirt onto his shoulders and thrust his arms though the sleeves and buttoned it, then found his britches at the foot of the bed and stood to draw them up over his slender hips. His fingers fumbled as he buttoned them. He had put on a few pounds during the winter. He didn't bother to light the lamp. Thus, partially dressed, he crept stealthily down the hallway to the water closet and took care of his early morning business.

The inside running hot water was a novelty to him. He turned on the faucet and let the liquid run for a moment to warm up. As he waited, he glanced at his face in the mirror. He scratched his scraggly beard and bared his straight white teeth. He put in the stopper, and when the sink was filled, took what he needed from his kit and began to shave. As he scraped the hair from his face, he contemplated the events of the last few days.

As manager of the Sweetwater Creek relay stage coach station, he'd heard rumors from the passengers of the near completion of the railroad into Denver from Cheyenne, and Joe knew with a sinking feeling in his stomach, that the days of the stage line were numbered. The facts were proven by the weekly newspaper that arrived on a Friday. He and his father, and the occupants of the station, had pored over the news and discussed it with foreboding. He decided to come to Denver and speak with the Western Division Agent personally about what effect it would have on his position as manager.

He left his father, Peter Hadley, and Slim, the animal handler, in charge of the animals and the station and hopped aboard the black coach to Denver, with the promise to return as soon as he could. He rode to Buckboard Station and spoke with Shadrach Weaver, manager of the station, about the matter of the completion of the railroad into Denver, while his wife, Bessie, served the meal to their guests. Shad agreed that the rail lines would bring changes to the route. Then, he took the red coach, with Rance Potter driving, to Rockland Station where he met John Moore, the new manager, for the first time and told him that he was going to speak with Wallace Tisdale about the horses he was planning to drive to Denver in the fall; he didn't tell either man of his real mission. Since neither station was an overnight stop, Joe was rushed from place to place with only time to eat and visit with his neighbors a short time, while the animal handlers changed the teams of horses.

He arrived at the Denver terminal in the late afternoon, collected his carpetbag from the rear boot, and said farewell to the driver and guard until the return trip to Sweetwater. He then walked across the street to an old, but clean and well-furnished hotel. He signed the register and paid the clerk for a three-night stay. The street noise outside his window seemed loud to his ears after the quiet of his home life. He had fallen asleep, tired and concerned about the reason for his visit to the bustling city.

He awoke early yesterday morning, ate a leisurely breakfast, and had plenty of time to visit with Wallace Tisdale, the agent for the Western Division of the Overland Stage line for which he worked, and catch up on the news of the town and the stage business. They discussed his reason for the trip, and Tisdale went with him to the telegraph office. While waiting for a response to the message, he walked the streets and explored a museum of American history. He laughed at some of the objects and frowned at others. He stopped in a mercantile store that Betty recommended and bought small gifts for his wife and mother. He found a set of miniature metal soldiers for Fuller that the store clerk assured him carried authentic copies of both

Napoleon's army, which were painted in blue, and that of the British, done up in red, about twenty-five total pieces in number, and a box of beads for Standing Tree's moccasins. In the evening, he ate a fine meal at the Tisdale home, and attended the opera in the Denver Theater they had read about in the papers, with Tisdale and his wife, Betty.

*****

Joe finished his business in the water closet and walked back to his room. He dressed in a clean shirt and trousers, with cotton socks on his feet. Holding his worn boot in his hands, he thought briefly of visiting a cobbler to see about new boots and shoes for his son, Fuller. But, they'd have to wait until he received a reply to his telegram from the home office of the stage line. He sighed, pulled on his boots and stood up. He cleaned up his room, donned his hat and went downstairs for his breakfast.

"Newspaper, sir?" A boy, not more than ten, had a stack of them in a sling over his shoulder. "It's the latest news, hot off the presses. Only a nickel."

"A nickel, huh?" Joe snorted, but he could see the boy hadn't sold many, and anyway, he might find some answers in the copy, if he could find a place to read it. He pulled out his change, sorted through several coins, and handed a thick one over in exchange for a copy of the paper. It did surprise him to see such a young child up so early, and in the lobby of the hotel. "Boy, shouldn't you be home in bed, so early in the morning?"

"No, sir. I got papers to sell." He looked past Joe and called to another early riser, "Newspaper, sir?"

Joe shrugged his shoulders; he'd been away from city life

for over three years. The noise and the smells were strange to him. If the newspaper companies wanted boys to sell their wares, and the boy's parents were willing, who was he to say anything? Holding the paper under his arm, he found a seat near the back of the restaurant and hung his hat on the rack on the wall.

When the waitress, a pert girl with short blonde hair arrived, he put his paper aside, calling out, "What sort of breakfast food do you have?"

"Just about what everyone serves. You won't find better, even if you pay more for your room. You just ask for what you want, and if we don't have it, I'll say so." She smiled, and she winked at him with one eye.

"Oh, you're good." He chuckled. "How about ham, eggs, fried potatoes, biscuits and coffee. You have that?"

"I believe so. You like your eggs runny or hard?"

"Cooked so they don't cluck." She laughed at that, and he watched her walk away, her hips swiveling in a provocative way. He laughed under his breath. If Hannah, his wife, had accompanied him, she would have slapped his face for his thoughts.

He spread his newspaper wide, and ignoring the headlines on the front page, turned to the back to where he was most interested. He had to flip several pages before he found what he wanted: the proposed schedule for the new railroad from Cheyenne to Denver, and the return to Cheyenne, with connecting stations to the East. He frowned. It was true; what had taken him and Hannah weeks to traverse, could now be done in a matter of days. His eyes searched for St. Louis, but it wasn't on the schedule. That pleased him. At least the stage lines were still running through the area where Ned Baldwin was the

Eastern Agent.

"Here, sir. You make room for this, and I'll bring you a second cup when you finish." A steaming cup of coffee appeared magically out of nowhere.

"Ah, you're a good girl. You better have that fresh cup ready. I'm about as thirsty as a horse that's not seen a trough in two days."

The waitress set his coffee off to the side, and she flounced away. He shook his head, wondering what else she did besides serve breakfast. Nothing he'd be interested in, for certain.

He was reminded of Baldwin and his wife and children as he sipped the hot brew. He heard a sound and recognized it as the waitress sighing. Had she hoped for a proposition from him? He ignored her, thinking of his Hannah and the start of the journey west. It had been three years since they had disembarked from the steamboat and ridden through the streets in Baldwin's carriage. He could remember it as though it were yesterday. The house had rung with the laughter and noise of small children, and Gladys, the eldest daughter, had grabbed Hannah's hat when the baby knocked it off her head. He remembered the eldest son holding a cigar behind his back in the study, hoping his father hadn't caught him smoking. Joe still periodically received letters from Ned, even though he was no longer his direct contact with the stage line officials. His son, Matthew, was now a driver for the line, as he had wanted. Gladys was happily married to a merchant in the town.

"Here." The waitress held a plate in each hand. "This is a mighty lot for one man."

"Not for a hungry man." Joe took one of the plates from her and made room on the table for the other one. He folded the newspaper and put it beside his plate while he ate his breakfast.

He glanced around at the other diners, some he recognized who were guests of the hotel. Others, by their dress, were local people on their way to work, he supposed. He had become a keen observer of men's and women's habits and character in his years as manager of the Sweetwater Station. He watched the waitress flirt with a lone male sitting at a corner table. Another man dressed in black suit and tie was looking closely at her, and Joe had time to wonder if he was jealous or displeased. Three women came in the door and marched to a table near the window, chattering like magpies. Their skirts billowed around them as they sat down; one of them had a hat with a stuffed bird. He chuckled to himself, as he thought of Standing Tree's assessment of women who wore stuffed birds on their hats.

He put his attention on his food, quickly finished and paid his bill. He pulled his hat low on his head as he left the restaurant and strode to the office of his boss. He stopped in front of the door of the building and glanced up and down the street. People shuffled along the sidewalks, their eyes focused on their own affairs, ignoring the other pedestrians as they went. City life was fine for some people, but he preferred the open air and the sight of the far distant mountains seen from his house in the forest. He sighed and opened the door.

Joe knew where to go from his visit the day before. His footsteps echoed in the hallway as he turned toward the stairs and took them with a bold stride. He gave a rare thought to the man who had visited him from Wells-Fargo in his first year at Sweetwater. He could have had an office like this; but he had chosen to continue at his own place among the towering pines and fragrant spruce of the forest.

The receptionist was standing, working at a counter, and she looked up when he walked in. She had dark hair and eyes, and wore a pale blue shirtwaist dress with a high white collar, decorated at the neck with a cameo pin encircled by silver filigree. She smiled.

"Good morning, Mr. Hadley. I hope it's a good one for you. Mr. Tisdale's busy right now. Would you take a chair and wait?" She pointed to the opposite wall, where three chairs were lined in a row.

Joe sat and looked around the room. A fly was buzzing at the window. He watched as it kept butting against the glass, trying to find a way out to the open air.

He didn't have long to wait. The man himself came out of the office with his hand outstretched.

"Ah, Joe, I see you have arrived in good time. Come in. Come in." He turned to the receptionist. "Clara, when you finish with the new schedule guide, take it to the printers and enjoy the afternoon off. I won't be returning to the office today. Buy yourself a new hat or something."

"Thank you, Mr. Tisdale, but I'll spend the time with my mother. She said yesterday that I need to come see her more often." She laughed and sat in her chair.

Joe followed his employer into his office and stood at attention.

"Joe, take a seat." Wallace closed the door and rounded his desk and sat in his leather seat behind it. He looked closely at Joe and laughed. "Well, you got what you wanted, although I was mighty surprised to see the telegram." He lifted a paper from his desk and handed it to Joe.

Joe gave him a speculative glance and read the telegram. "Offer accepted. Stop. Hadley approved for sale; price to be negotiated. Stop. Will contact Colorado governor personally. Dempsey."

12

Joe sat stunned, trying to take it in. His eyes stung with unshed tears. He looked across at Tisdale and smiled. "I can have it? Really? I can't wait to tell Hannah. Oh, God. I didn't dream it would work."

"Then you should be very happy. What made you choose to stay, even though the rail lines are taking over the country?" Tisdale seemed sincerely interested.

Joe sat back, unaccountably pleased with the question. "Mostly for my parents. I want them to have security for the rest of their lives; and, what better place to live than Sweetwater Springs? When I came back from the war, my father had become a drunk; my mother was despondent over the death of my older brother, James. It was a bad time." He laughed. "It was the best day of my life when Rusty Backgammon opened the door of the stage and my parents stepped onto Colorado soil."

"I'm glad the stage facilities won't be abandoned. Someone might as well get use of what we built out there." Tisdale rapped the surface of his desk with a chuckle.

Joe rose, too filled with anticipation to sit, and he walked around the room before coming back to his employer. "Thank you, Wallace; this is a glorious day to be alive."

"Well, there are still the formalities to take care of, you know." He pulled his timepiece from his pocket and looked at the time. "We've barely time to get to the capitol before our meeting with the governor. Come, Joe, it's a short walk and will give you time to collect your thoughts."

The two men departed the building that housed the Denver offices of the Overland Stage Lines and strode briskly to the Territorial Capitol Building. Tisdale seemed to know exactly where he was going, and Joe was grateful, for he was walking on air.

He'd approached the agent with some trepidation when he'd first come up with the idea of buying the land and accruements of the stage station, most of which he had built with his own hands. Like old Daniel in the Bible, he had already read the handwriting on the wall and knew the stage lines would be discontinued when the railroads were built. If he owned the land and buildings, he could continue to live on the property until he decided to move on. He hoped the stage would continue to run through his property but, the future was uncertain. And if by some chance he and Hannah were transferred to another station; at least, his parents could remain at Sweetwater and have the security they deserved. Hannah had agreed it was a good plan and gave her approval for his use of much of her remaining inheritance for the purchase.

The meeting with the governor was short, and Joe was honored to have had the chance to meet such a prestigious dignitary. They shook hands, and he and Tisdale visited the land office, where the helpful clerk searched for and found the spot on the map where his station stood. With the approval of the stage authorities and the governor, he purchased the land and accruements already built on the land. The fields and the gardens, the spring and the creek on both banks, and one hundred acres were now his own, free and clear of mortgage or debt. The farthest boundary to the northwest included twenty-five acres along the river, assuring him access to the fishing rights where his father and Standing Tree found their greatest pleasure and a source of food for the diets of the residents.

He departed the building with a big smile on his face and the official papers in the leather satchel held tightly in his hand. He left Tisdale and strolled to a local livery, where he rented a horse and rode to the end of the tracks. There he sat on the horse to gawk at the sight of his enemy, as though he were again a member of the Southern Army under General Morgan. He watched as the giant engine puffed to a water tower, and men scrambled to fill the boiler. He sat for a time, observing the action and frowned. Finally, resigned to his fate, he turned the horse and left the scene, knowing that it was a matter of time before the hulking metal dragons would be crossing the country and the stage line would be gone. Leaving the livery stable, he felt reassured as he hefted his leather satchel and patted its side.

He ate a hearty evening meal provided by Betty's housekeeper and cook. He washed it down with a glass of red wine, the first taste of liquor since he took on the position of stage station manager. Betty put the children to bed early, and Joe and Tisdale gathered in the parlor for a friendly game of cards. Noticing the time on the mantle clock, he rose to take his leave.

"I can't thank you enough, Wallace, for your help in this matter. You have been a true friend. My parents will have a secure home for the rest of their lives." Joe stretched out his hand to his superior, but Tisdale demurred.

"Joe, don't thank me. I did nothing but send telegrams. It was John Dempsey who had influence over the stockholders of the company. He has a great deal of respect for you. He also consulted with a man named Bowman, a stockholder, I understand. He also has a high regard for your character. I'm not supposed to tell you that; but I feel the wind is blowing in the wrong direction; if they lay tracks into Trinidad and towns south, long-distance stage travel is doomed. I might be out of a job myself in a few years. Good-bye, Joe. Take care of that boy of yours." He walked with Joe to the door, shook hands one last time, and shut the door when Joe had disappeared from sight.

Joe made a second visit to the opera house alone, and early the next morning checked out of his hotel. He was waiting at the stage terminal when Rance Potter and his guard, Thad Ray, drove up with the team of horses for the trip to Buckboard Station.

"Rance!" Joe waved an arm.

"Well, ain't this something, one of the bosses taking a ride on my stage?" Rance elbowed Thad in the side, and he chortled.

"Better make this a good trip, Rance. I'm in with the higher ups, now." Joe ribbed him with a laugh.

"Ain't nobody higher up than me." Rance patted the seat next to him. "Not unless'n they choose to sit up here with me."

Thad broke into laughter, but by then, Joe was inside, and Rance called, "How-town honeys! Get yourselves up and on the road." With that, he cracked his whip, and the stage jerked forward.

After Rance's leg of the journey came to an end, Joe wished the two men well and transferred to the black coach with Ivan Mandrake and Hank Philips for the last leg of his journey to Sweetwater.

There were two women and three men in the coach. Joe soon found that one of the men, Adam Roe, was brother to one of the women, Delta Flint, traveling with her husband, Salton Flint. Roe's wife, Tonya, timidly held out her hand, while holding a handkerchief over her mouth and nose to keep out the dust. The other man, Ambrosine, gazed out the window as they left the station.

"Have you ridden the stage before?" The question came from Adam and was directed to Joe. Ambrosine turned from the window with a glance of curiosity.

"Other than the one you were just on." Delta smiled, and

her eyes glinted with amusement.

"A time or two." Joe didn't say more, as they might very well be staying at his station when they arrived. He didn't want to become too friendly with people who might be under his care. For the rest of the trip, they discussed the pleasant weather, the election of the former Army general, Ulysses S. Grant, to the presidency and whether the railroad would be extended south to Santa Fe in New Mexico Territory. The ladies were more interested in women's suffrage. Salton Flint agreed with his wife and sister-in-law. The traveling salesman in their group, Ambrosine, didn't take offense at the views, but joined in the conversation. Joe listened carefully to their talk, and thought to ask his wife and mother about the subject later.

As the drone of voices continued, Joe sat on the comfortable maroon velvet seat and thought of Jeremiah Fuller, and his sacrifice for him. He gazed out the window at the scenery and tears filled his eyes. He quickly and secretly brushed them aside, blaming the dust from the road for the watery eyes.

Jeremiah Fuller had fought on the side of the Southern Rebels during the late war. He'd been a student at the University in Tennessee when war broke out, and had come home to find his parents and young sister dead of the cholera epidemic that spread through his town. His brothers had been off fighting the war, and he had joined up for the duration.

After the war, he had taken several temporary jobs and ended up as drover with Brodie White on the freight caravan that brought supplies to Sweetwater Station and the other stations from St. Louis to Denver. Joe chuckled as he remembered the first day he met Jeremiah, fresh-faced and eager to please. But, the day had quickly taken on serious undertones as Brodie White, drunk and arrogant, pulled his gun on Buck Jones, the station's animal handler. Buck killed the man, and Joe had asked Jeremiah to stay as his hired hand, to help with building the barn and outbuildings. Their friendship had grown during the months that followed.

It was when the new Concord stages came onto the station grounds that trouble came to the forest at the base of the Rocky Mountains, for Dakota had arrived as guard and shotgun messenger on the black coach and Bruno Smith as the driver. It was the same day that Rance Potter and his guard Thad Ray had arrived on the red coach. In the weeks after his arrival, Dakota started drinking and gambling when they visited the Buckboard Station.

Coming back from a trip to the Mozier station, with Bruno driving and Dakota on the seat beside him, they had quarreled; and as Joe and Jeremiah stood at the corrals waiting for the stage, Dakota leaped from the coach, his pistol pointed at Joe. Jeremiah deflected the lethal bullet and lost his life in protecting his employer. Bruno had killed Dakota, and the two men were laid to rest in the tall pine trees near the mound that contained the body of Brodie White. Joe often visited the gravesite, and Hannah or Ruth took flowers to place at the grave on the anniversary of his death. As Joe gazed out of the coach, focused on his thoughts, he was startled by a rising argument between the passengers inside the coach.

"You just wait, young man, until the women have the vote; then you'll see a change in Washington." Delta's cheeks were flushed, and it seemed she could barely contain her fury.

Joe, coming out of his haze of recollection couldn't recall what had started the flare-up but, he watched as Adam Roe, red-faced and embarrassed, turned from his angry sister.

Ambrosine tried to calm the situation, speaking in a gentle

and soothing voice. "Well, ma'am, we all agree that when General Grant becomes president, he'll have some control over the Congress. He's a war hero, and people will listen to him."

"Hah, War Mongers, all of them. Can't see beyond the nose on their face. Someday, there'll be a woman president and the wars will stop, and the prophesy of Micah in the Bible will come true."

"And, what prophesy might that be, ma'am?" asked the mild-mannered Ambrosine.

"Why, that the plowshares will be turned into pruning forks, and men will train for war no more." The lady huffed and blew out her cheeks. She lifted her hand to straighten her bonnet, a black affair with a sprig of colorful flowers in the brim.

Flint cleared his throat, and gently chastised his wife. "Now, dear, these people are tired. Why don't you rest a moment, and enjoy the ride?" She gave him a seething glance from the corner of her eye but stopped talking.

After a while, Tonya Roe speculated on what they would be served for their evening meal, and Joe grinned to himself. There were no more arguments or discussion about politics through the rest of the trip.

His heart leapt with joy and pride when Ivan Mandrake drove the last mile through the forest and onto his grounds. He grinned for no reason except his secret knowledge that the land was his own. The stage stopped with a flourish, and Joe suspected that Ivan was attempting to show off his expertise. He laughed at the expressions on the faces of the ladies. The door was opened by his father. The passengers swept from the coach, and Joe exited, the last to do so. He looked toward the house, saw the beautiful face of his wife and gazed around him with a slight frown when he saw that Slim wasn't on hand. He shrugged it aside and listened as the passengers were welcomed and invited to join the family for a meal in the Public Room.

He neither knew, nor cared what the passengers thought when he drew Hannah into his arms and gave her a smack on her damaged cheek. She gave a small gasp of alarm, and responded with a laugh of pleasure.

"Hello, darling. What have you prepared for our dinner? I'm hungry enough to eat a mule."

She gave him a cuff on the arm and turned aside to lead the women into the house. "Please come in, ladies, and I'll serve tea as soon as you are settled in your rooms. Don't be alarmed. This is my husband, who has been on a business trip to Denver." She smiled at the expressions of relief on the women's faces. Ivan and Hank Philips, the guard, began to take the luggage from the rear boot and line it up on the porch.

Standing Tree came to welcome him and began to talk swiftly in his language. Joe could make out something about a bear. He turned to Peter and raised an eyebrow.

"Yes, son, he saw a bear near the spring early yesterday morning. He wanted to follow it, but I told him to wait until you got back. We followed the tracks for a few yards into the forest, but lost them near that stand of spruce trees and boulders. You remember the place where we camped during our recent mustang hunt. I told Slim and the coachmen to keep a sharp lookout for the animal."

"We'll wait until our guests are gone on their way and see about tracking the bear again. I'm tired, and I can now appreciate the visit to the station from the passenger's point of view more clearly. I'll wash up and eat a bite, make sure the men guests are settled and look around. Where's Slim?" He looked toward the barn and corrals.

"He's in the barn with one of the goats. He came too close to the fence and knocked several poles down and tried to run away. His flank is scratched, and Slim is tending to the wound with his evil-smelling salves. Dumb animals; the goats are never satisfied with the bushes and vines to hand; they always want the ones on the other side of the fence." He turned to go into the house.

Joe watched as the coachmen unhitched the team and took them to the water trough. Ivan began checking them for mouth sores or abrasions from the harness rubbing the flesh. Satisfied that they were following his unspoken instructions, he mounted the steps and entered his home, where he was immediately assaulted by a barking dog and flying boy who grabbed him around the legs and almost toppled him over.

"Papa. Papa. Up. Up," the boy demanded, and Joe set his luggage on the floor and lifted him high into the air and brought him down to hug him tightly.

"What have you been doing in my absence?" He pinched the boy's cheek, laughing as he did so.

"Play'n'." He put his hand in Joe's hair and pulled. "Higher, Papa."

Joe laughed at the boy and gave him a kiss before setting him on his feet; and he ran to Standing Tree who gathered him closely in his arms, his blanket falling to the floor.

Joe was hardly aware of the guests as he strolled through the room and hallway to his bedroom, his leather satchel in one hand and the carpetbag in the other, the dog following at his heels. He gazed at the comfortable bed and wished he could lie down for a nap, but knew he couldn't. He put the luggage into the closet notch out of sight to be dealt with later, and removed his jacket. He rolled his shirt sleeves to the elbows and washed his face and hands, and dried them with the flannel towel. All the experiences of the last hour were new to him; seeing and hearing the activities of the station from the passengers' point of view. How easy it had been to forget in the three years since he and Hannah had left his parents' farm in Indiana and traveled by steamboat and stage to this isolated way station near the mountains. He looked at Jack sitting on his tail beside the bed. He opened the door, and the dog escaped into the hallway to run to the Public Room.

Joe sat on the bed and took off his leather boots and put his more comfortable moccasins on his feet. As he moved, his thoughts drifted to the sighting of the bear by the Indian. He frowned. He'd become complacent, he realized, living in the confines of the station fence. He'd almost forgotten the wildness of the area. He determined to talk to his employees about the continued necessity of posting night guards.

When Joe returned to the Public Room, it was in his role as manager of the station. He greeted his companions from the stage formally.

"Mr. Roe, and your attractive wife, Mrs. Roe." When she held out her hand, he took it and gave it a short shake. He turned to the other three guests. "Mr. Flint, welcome, and to your wife, also. And Mr. Ambrosine, I appreciate your soothing words on the trip down. If you'll join us for our meal, you won't regret my wife's cooking."

If the guests were surprised, they didn't say. Joe took his place at the head of the table and Hannah brought his coffee. Fuller was sitting in his tall chair, a spoon in his hand. The tureen of soup was in the center of the table.

"Bowls. Please, one at a time." Hannah stood back from the table, indicating each person should take what they wanted. Joe dipped the ladle first, filled his bowl and began to eat. The other guests followed suit, and soon, freshly baked bread was passed around.

"This smells wonderful!" Delta Flint lifted her spoon and sipped the broth. "Oh! It tastes even better!"

"And I shall expect such excellent fare when we reach the end of our journey, my good wife." Mr. Flint winked at Joe, and he smiled.

His wife just laughed, poking her husband on the arm with an extended finger.

When the soup was finished, Ruth set the roast in front of Joe's plate, and he stood to carve small slices, as though he had never been away. The platter was passed around the table; and the bowls of boiled potatoes, mustard greens, corn, and finally, slices of yellow cake with boiled icing made of egg whites.

In a break in the conversation, Standing Tree stood and with his usual deep, basal voice announced, "Yo Hadley come back. We glad. He and Scarred Woman my friends. Big Father come from across mighty river. He like smoke. Yo Hadley not like smoke; but fine fellow." He looked at the men and circled the table, and Joe was forced to rise. His hand was pumped up and down several times, and Standing Tree walked out the door.

Leaving the guests to the expertise of the women and his father, Joe rose from the table and went to see Slim about the injured goat. The dog tagged along beside him. It felt good to breathe the air, even as the smell of wood smoke and cooked meat mingled with the aroma of the pine forest. It was home, and Joe looked to the mountains, and smiled. He didn't see Standing Tree and assumed he was in the outhouse. He started off at a brisk pace to the goat enclosure. Slim wasn't there; so he opened the door of the barn. He could see the light from the doctor's surgery space and went to him, whistling so he wouldn't frighten the man, coming up to him from the passage.

"Hello, Joe. Be with you in a minute." It was a welcome sound, to hear the animal handler's voice. Joe moved toward the sound. He saw Slim, standing at the head of the goat lying on the large table where he tended to the smaller animals.

"Can he be saved?" Joe watched as Slim rubbed his evil-smelling salve onto the long scratch on the goat's side. He looked at Slim's face and saw the sweat on his forehead. He grabbed a clean cloth from the shelf and wiped it off for him. It was a ritual he had performed before. He frowned at the stillness of the animal.

"Don't know. Time will tell; but it's a bad wound. I don't like the way he's breathing, shallow and labored."

Joe looked at the animal. He hadn't noticed but could see since it was brought to his attention, the fast rise and fall of the goat's mid-section. Slim turned away and clamped the lid onto the tin of salve, and placed it on the shelf above the table. Joe felt a twinge of pride, for he had built the shelf himself for the veterinarian's use.

Slim sighed, and it carried the note of a man who was exhausted past endurance.

"Why don't you go eat your dinner? Got a table full of guests tonight. What do I need to do while you're gone to help the animal?"

"Just keep him quiet, if you can. I won't stay long. Was your trip successful?"

Neither Slim nor the coachmen knew why Joe went to Denver. He had told them it was about the station business; something he wanted to consult with Tisdale about and didn't want to write it in a letter

Joe decided to let his handler think it concerned his fear of losing their positions with the stage line, if the railroad tracks were nearly to Denver from Cheyenne.

"The railroad is only a few miles from Denver; I saw it. You know what that means, Slim, an end to the cross-country stage lines. I wanted to discuss it with Tisdale. I knew from the beginning that once the war was over; the officials in Washington City and New York would start laying tracks across the prairies. With General Grant president, the Union Pacific and the Central Pacific will meet in Utah, maybe next month. Once the tracks are finished, the people will have a faster and safer way across the country." He took off his hat and scratched his head. He shrugged and put it back. "That doesn't affect us here for now; people will still need access to Trinidad and Pueblo, but the northern cross-country routes will be closed. Don't mention what I've said to the guests, although Ivan and Hank will soon need to know. All our jobs are in jeopardy. I'm sorry. I don't have better news than that."

"Are you saying that we should start thinking about leaving Sweetwater?"

"Don't do anything rash. I asked Tisdale, and he seemed to think the stage will continue for at least another year, but you know, with the tracks into Denver, some enterprising men will look to the south and west toward Santa Fe. For now, it's best to just do our jobs as well we can. Papa said that Standing Tree sighted a bear in the woods. That's more important to us than railroad tracks. Go eat your supper. Don't worry. I need you here." He put a comforting hand on the man's shoulder and gave him a smile.

"Thanks, Joe. I'll sure hate to leave this place. I'm glad you've given me a chance to earn my pay. When I first came here, you seemed so young, and I wasn't sure we'd get along. Baldwin told me you'd fought for the Confederacy. I'd built up a mighty hatred for you rebels." He grinned. "'Course Hannah's good cooking helped a lot towards a truce between North and South. I still remember that first supper with the other folks, and Standing Tree proclaiming his allegiance to you. I've grown to love that old Indian. He's slowing down, Joe, but he's still strong enough for a few more years. How old do you think he is?" The men had started walking down the corridor to the front of the barn.

"I'd say at least in his sixties, just guessing. His village tossed him out like an old bone. I wish I could speak his language better. He probably has some interesting tales to tell. Go eat; I'll stay with the goat." Joe stood in the open door of the barn and watched as Slim walked to the house and entered it. He sighed and went back to the surgery part of the barn. He found a ladder back chair, sat down and leaned against the wall.

He suddenly came wide awake when he heard two men laughing, and looked up to see Ivan and Hank in the doorway. He gave them a sheepish grin. Standing behind them was Slim, with a straw in his mouth, his eyes twinkling.

"Look'ee there, Ivan. 'Tain't often we catch the boss napping. Must have been all that carousing he done in Denver. Say, Boss, were there purty girls in the big city?" Hank teased.

"Of course, there were, Hank. I saw some singing on the stage at the opera house. Went there twice." He became serious. "Are the animals quiet? I should go to them, but I haven't the strength of mind. Come on to the bunkhouse and I'll fill you in on my trip." The men waited for Slim to check on the goat, and they all tramped to the large room in the bunkhouse, where they spent a pleasant half-hour discussing the merits of the city life.

Joe didn't say anything to the coachmen about his business with Tisdale, and Slim kept silent about their futures. Hank would take the first watch; Joe cautioned him about the bear sighting; told him to keep his rifle handy. He finally wished them good-night and went to the house.

The night was calm, and a slightly slanted moon shone down on the station, lighting his way across the yard. He spoke to Standing Tree as he passed his tree. The man was squatting on the ground, smoking his pipe. They spoke for a few minutes in the disjointed part-English, part-sign language to which they had grown accustomed. He said good-night and entered the house, where Hannah waited for him, with the dog asleep next to the rocking chair.

He made sure the coals in the fireplace were contained, and held out his hand, "Come, my dear." Hannah rose and followed him to the bedroom. They undressed in the semi-darkness with only the light from the moon showing through the window. They remained quiet for a few minutes, and Joe began to tell her about the trip. When he assured her that the land and buildings were now their own, and she would never have to worry about her home, she began to cry. He comforted her, and with the skill earned through years of love for his mate, they began to talk of their feelings for each other. Finally, exhausted both physically and spiritually, the couple slept through the night. The dog occasionally sniffled or moved during the night, but didn't awaken them.

Two

Hannah arose before dawn and went outside to breathe in the cool mountain air. She gathered several pine cones from the ground under a tree. She watched as Jack bounded about on his short legs and barked at a bird. She returned to the house and began to put kindling and the pine cones in the stove. They gave off a pleasant smell. She heard the boy whimper and went to get him, hoping not to awaken Joe; but her husband was already at the baby's cot, patting Fuller on the back.

"I'm sorry, dear, I don't think he's going back to sleep. I'll dress and bring him into the Public Room; you take care of your chores. The guests will be up soon, and I need to talk to Slim about the wounded goat."

"That's fine, honey. I thought I'd make sweet rolls this morning; the guests seem to like them. Would you bring in some wood if you have time? The box is getting low." Hannah turned to the kitchen without waiting for Joe to answer. The dog watched her a moment and lay down beside the fireplace.

Joe chuckled under his breath and began to dress for the day. He left his torso bare until he had shaved. With his shirt in one hand and the sleepy boy in his arms, he entered the kitchen area in time to see Hannah pulling tins from a high shelf. He put the boy in his tall chair and gave him a spoon to play with; and reaching for the dipper, poured some hot water into the pail on the table. Standing where he could keep an eye on Fuller, he shaved and dried his face with a clean flannel towel. He heard a noise and saw his mother coming from the bedroom. His father staggered behind her, his hair still rumpled and his eyes half-asleep.

"Good morning, all. Did you sleep well?" Without waiting for an answer, Joe glanced around the room to see if anyone else had come in, and continued. "Papa, Mama, the stage authorities approved my request. You wouldn't remember William Bowman, but Hannah does. He and the other stock holders and John Dempsey gave permission for me to buy the property on which you stand."

He grinned as he waited for a reaction. Peter gasped, Ruth gazed at him in shock and Hannah threw a slice of bacon in the skillet and laughed, as Fuller banged on his chair with his spoon.

"Papa, you and Standing Tree can go fishing in the river anytime you like; your favorite spot belongs to us now." He looked out the window, where the new sun could be seen through the trees. "It's all ours, the land, the buildings, the forest and the springs."

Walking toward him, Peter grasped Joe around the neck, and releasing him, he took his coat off the peg. Without a word, he walked out the door. Joe watched him, a puzzled look on his face.

"Don't mind him, son; he's happy. I'm so pleased. You're a kind, thoughtful son, and I love you." Joe held his mother for a minute until she dried her eyes and moved to the stove to help Hannah cook breakfast.

"I love you, too, Mama, and Papa, as well. I'm thinking when the traffic slacks off a bit we might add a couple of rooms to the house, so we'll have more space. What do you think, Hannah, upstairs or down?"

"Oh, Joe, that would be fine. If you could build on, we'd have more rooms for the guests. And, Fuller could have a room of his own." She took the coffee off the stove and poured him a cup. She had a dreamy look in her eyes, and Joe grinned.

"Well, I'll get to it when we can, but first we have to feed the guests and help them on their way. Mama, I'll bring in more wood for the fire." He swallowed the last of his coffee, lifted his rifle from the shelf and took his hat and coat from the pegs by the door, and went out. He stood for a moment on the porch and saw the light in the bunkhouse, and he knew that Slim and the stage hands were up and getting dressed. He watched his father approach with a bucket of milk in his hand.

"I'll bring in some wood, Papa," he said as he passed him in the yard. His father nodded and went into the house.

In the two years since Peter Hadley had been at Sweetwater Creek, Joe had watched his father change in many ways. From the sad, drunken sot he had found when he returned from the war, Peter had regained his strength and sense of self-worth. Joe was certain it came from the open air, the sense of responsibility in helping with the station work and his pride in the kitchen garden and fields of golden corn, wheat and oats he tended across the creek from the house and barn.

His mother, Ruth, suffered from the pain in her hands from the progression of the disease that daily attacked her joints and knuckles, but her attitude was cheerful and her joy abounded when she held her grandson in her arms. She helped Hannah as best she could, and welcomed the overnight guests to the station with a smile of contentment. They hadn't heard from his older brother Luther since their arrival, and Joe knew his mother felt the loss of two of her sons. His brother, James, a Union soldier, had not returned from the war.

Joe knew the same feeling of pride and satisfaction, as he went for an armload of kindling. He took the ax from the log and started chopping wood, the sound ringing through the forest as he worked. When he had a considerable pile, he took the kindling and small chips in a bucket in the house and dumped it in the wood box. He saw that his father was sitting near the fireplace, smoking a cigar. He paused for a moment, watching the smoke rising around him before calling out.

"Papa, are you pleased?"

"Depends." He looked at his cigar and tapped some ashes on a rough piece of bark. Once the bark was full, he would toss it in the fire and pull another from the wood box. It was an equitable method that didn't waste any usable supplies, and neither did it cause any extra cleaning chores for the women.

"How's that?" Joe chuckled. It seemed it was all good to him.

"Remembering your brother. Soon's he got control of the family farm, he didn't want us around no more. Wondering how you might feel in six months' time." Joe's father didn't look at him as he spoke.

"Papa, this is your home."

"Supposing you and Hannah get a transfer to another station? I pay attention, better than you think. I know the railroads are coming through. Stations will get fewer, and only the best of the managers will stay on. They'll want you where they need you."

"Oh, Papa. That's why I bought the land and buildings. If that ever happens, you and Mama will be able to stay and keep the place for us until we return. This is your home always. Haven't you seen in the past three years I'm nothing like Luther?"

"Thought you needing my help had something to do with my welcome here." Papa cleared his throat, but his eyes had turned red. He tapped off his ashes again and took a draw on his cigar.

Joe laughed and clapped his father on the shoulder. "Papa, your help is appreciated every day. I couldn't run this station so well without you. It's you I love, and no matter what the coach lines do, this is your home always. Always, got that?"

"Thank you, son." His father's voice was gruff, but his eyes were moist as he turned to poke at the fire.

Joe rose and went out for more wood, following Jack as he ran down the steps in front of him. He raced to the tree where Standing Tree slept and barked.

Standing Tree rose from his bed under the tree; he spoke sharply to the barking dog, motioning for it to go away. In spite of his best efforts, Joe couldn't get the Indian to sleep in the bunkhouse except in extreme weather. The man liked the open skies and the freedom of movement provided by the wide outdoors. Joe remembered what Rosie Jones, the Apache wife of Buck, his first animal handler had said. The Indian still had a keen sense of hearing for his age, and was able to detect if intruders were nearby, either man or beast.

"Yo Hadley, we go for bear tracks? Yes?"

"Not right away; need to get the guests started on their way; two-three days, maybe. Go eat; stage coach comes today;

maybe more people. Then we hunt bear."

The Indian grunted and walked toward the house, the dog following closely beside him. Joe grinned and picked up an armful of kindling and a few pine cones.

When he returned to the Public Room, he noticed that the guests were eating breakfast. He unloaded the wood, and gave a nod to the guests. If they were surprised at him doing manual chores at the station, they didn't say. He sat and turned to one of the women at his side.

"Did you sleep well?" It was an innocuous question, one appropriate for the manager of a station, and when no answer was quickly forthcoming, he looked to one of the men across the table. "Any complaints about the accommodations?"

"One."

The response was from Mr. Roe, and it caught Joe off guard. He glanced at him to see a smile on the man's face.

"Do you wish to share it with me?" Joe looked up as Hannah placed a plate containing a steaming sweetroll before him and stepped away. She wore a smile of her own, but shook her head and stepped back to the stove. Joe prompted, "Mr. Roe?"

The other passengers at the table seemed to be in on the joke. Mrs. Flint spoke up first.

"We were assured we would be treated to the most delicious apple pie when we reached Sweetwater Station. Your wife's sweetrolls, they are quite delicious, but, well, you see our predicament. Our mouths were watering for pie, and it's just not the same."

"I assured them," Hannah called from the far side of the room, "that on their next visit, I would have enough dried fruit in reserve to serve each person a generous slice."

"Ah, so you will be coming back?" Joe was grinning by

then. At the vigorous nods around the table, he turned to his plate, ate a sweetroll and a bowl of hot porridge Hannah had placed alongside it, and finished his coffee. With a nod to the other diners, he rose and plucked his hat off the peg by the door.

Coming from the house Joe looked to his right, where under the shingled roof, the black stage coach stood waiting to take the passengers from Sweetwater to Rockland Station, or in reverse from Rockland to Sweetwater, where they would be driven by Rusty Backgammon to their eastern destinations, or south by Jim Owens. The coach was no longer shiny and new, but slightly battered with a large scratch along one side caused by a too close contact with a tree branch. The soft velvet seats were rumpled and stained in one place, where a careless miner had spilt his bottle of liquor. Joe grinned when he remembered the day he had first seen it. It had been accompanied by a second coach; red in color, driven by Rance Potter. It was still used between the Buckboard Station and Denver.

The salesman, Ambrosine, followed him to the corral, where six stout mules were waiting to be hitched to the black coach for the trip to Mozier. He turned when the salesman spoke from behind him.

"Mr. Hadley, my business is men's wear; I work for a tailor's shop in Denver. I have a catalog of our line in my bag, if you and your men would care to see the latest style in men's suits. We carry some fine ties made from China silk." He stopped talking and looked around him. Joe had lifted the log that served as a corral gate, and stepped into the pen, and was looking at the hoof of one of the mules. Out of the corner of his eye, he saw Ivan leave the bunkhouse and walk toward them.

"Of course, you may have no need for fine wool suits in the wilderness; but a man's got to make a living." He shrugged and muttered, "Good morning, sir," to Ivan, who held the harness in his hand, the reins thrown over his shoulder.

"Ivan, this is Mr. Ambrosine. He sells fine wool suits for men. You have need of a new suit?" He put the harness on the mules while Ivan held them by the lead rope. He led the mules out into the open by their harness reins. Ivan gawked at the salesman as if he had three heads.

"Suits? What the hell would I want with a suit, driving the coach and all?" He swatted the rear of one of the mules, a stubborn cuss that they often had trouble with of a morning. He and Joe took the team to the black coach and began to hitch them to the vehicle. When Ivan was finished, Joe turned to the salesman.

"I tell you what, Mr. Ambrosine, you get out your catalog, and I'll talk to you before you leave. Right now, we have a job to do." Joe watched as Ivan rose to the box, and releasing the brake, guided the mules across the yard to stand waiting for the guests to finish their meal.

Ambrosine ran to the bunkhouse where he had slept in a spare room and collected his belongings. He took his thin paper catalog out of his bag, entered the house and stood beside the table in the Public Room, his hands trembling with nervousness. Hannah looked at him and finished clearing the table. Roe and his wife rose and went into their room for their bags. Flint and his wife were talking to Ruth when Joe entered the room.

Joe took it all in with one glance and frowned, certain that the woman was trying to get his mother to join their women's suffrage movement. He stepped to them and said, "Mama, is everything alright over here?"

"Now, Mr. Hadley, don't be thinking we're trying to coerce anyone into anything." Flint patted his pockets and pulled out a

35

round timepiece with a great winding knob on the top. It had a cover, and he pressed something to pop it open. He barely looked at it before slipping it back into his pocket. "Mother, maybe we should begin moving our bags to the door."

"I'm sure that will be a good idea," Joe suggested. "The coach will be leaving in fifteen minutes." He turned as Hank came in to eat his breakfast, his shotgun in his left arm. He was late, and Joe wondered what had held him up, but he would wait to question him on their return from Mozier's station. The passengers wandered out to the coach, and Ivan lifted their luggage into the rear boot.

"Mr. Ambrosine, I have a minute if you would care to show me your catalog." He watched and listened politely while the man turned pages; one of the displays caught his eye. He glanced around to see if Peter was nearby, but his father had gone outside. He told the salesman to wait.

"Mama, look at this suit. Do you think that Papa might like it for his birthday?" Ruth nodded her head in answer and turned away to start the cleaning up.

Hannah came over. "What are you showing Ruth?"

"Something for Papa." Joe pointed to the illustration.

"That is very thoughtful of you, Joe. I'm sure he would like that very much. Is there anything for small boys?"

"Oh, certainly, ma'am." Ambrosine was flushed, as if he couldn't believe his good fortune, and he turned to the back of the catalog. She looked at several illustrations and pointed to one.

"Joe, do you like this one?" She tapped it with her finger.

"Shall we ask Fuller's opinion?" Joe caught the salesman's eyes, and he smiled.

"You're a silly man. A child has no opinion. I like it. That's the one." Hannah huffed and turned back to her chores.

"How would we get the items? Do they come in the mail bag?" Joe was usually not impulsive but recognized an opportunity when it came. In spite of her casual dismissal of Fuller's input, Hannah seemed eager for a suit of clothes for their son, and even Joe realized how nice it would be for the women not to have to make every item the boy wore.

Ambrosine got out his pencil and order form and wrote down their selection. Joe handed him the amount specified in the catalog, by then considering that he didn't know anything about the man, and now thinking he'd probably not see the suits or the money again. He sighed and told the salesman to move along to the coach.

Hank left the table, coffee dripping from his chin. He wiped it off with his handkerchief and went out to climb aboard the stage. Joe followed more slowly and turned to inspect the wagon wheels and axles. He moved quickly to the mules and waved for Ivan to proceed. The driver climbed into the box, and with a creak of leather, the mules stepped out lively and the wheels began to roll away from the station.

As soon as the coach was gone, Joe and Peter saddled horses, and with Standing Tree beside them on his mount, with his bow and quiver of arrows on his back, started off to find the bear tracks. They rode toward the river and followed the bank for a few miles, but the Indian found no sign of tracks or fur shrugged off against a tree or bush. They circled to come back along the road through the forest, but no sign was found. They turned back to the station, both disappointed and relieved. Joe was determined to set a guard out at night, but no bear was sighted near the station or fence.

Three

Two days after returning from Denver, Joe walked to the corrals to greet Slim, his animal handler. He paused a moment in the damp air, seeing his home wrapped in a fog that had gathered over the spring and creek. The station hardly resembled the place where he and Hannah had first appeared as host and hostess of the overnight stop of the Overland Stage Company.

The large brick barn that Joe had built with the aid of his hired hand, Jeremiah Fuller, was now covered on one side by moss and another side by climbing vines. The two end walls held double doors, and the inside contained horse stalls and Slim's surgery and equipment, and it smelled of medicines and vinegar. Slim Grimshaw was a fully-trained veterinarian and animal handler, hired by the stage company. The loft was piled high with bags of grain and hay stored for the animals.

Next to the stage shelter and joined by the same roof was the large building that housed the unmarried station workers and coach drivers on their layover between trips. He and his father had built eight compartments, with a large open area with a huge fireplace for the men to relax when not working. Behind the bunkhouse stood a row of sheds, housing the goats and leaving them enough open space to browse on the vines and shrubs at the edge of the forest. Next to it stood the hen house. The two roosters crowed and flapped their wings in competition for the loudest welcome of the early morning. Joe laughed at them.

He held a sense of affection for the bunkhouse, for he remembered clearly the day he had returned from his first mustang hunt, to be escorted by Jeremiah around the building and inside the hollow shell, built by McKinley, who had brought the two new coaches from the East. He paused, with a frown on his brow, to think of that day that seemed so long ago. His glance instinctively rose to the half-hidden mounds on the slight rise above the fog-enclosed spring. He couldn't remember that day without thoughts of the young Confederate soldier from Tennessee who had given his life to save him. He remembered the grin on the man's face as he extolled the virtues of the building's fireplace, walls, and dirt floor.

Joe saw two men come out of the building, and he quickly put thoughts of the past behind him as he crossed to greet them. From the corner of his eye, he saw Standing Tree walking toward the house. The man seemed to be limping, but Joe didn't have time to consider the matter.

"Good morning, men; looks to be a fine day for a trip. As soon as you eat, we'll separate the horses for the coach. Ivan, check that left front wheel again. We may have to replace it before you leave. I'm going to speak with Slim and join you at the corral. Hannah's got her famous sweet rolls instead of biscuits this morning. Coffee's hot." He tipped his hat and they left him with smiles on their faces.

39

Joe had first met Ivan Mandrake when he took Rusty Backgammon's place years ago, when the old timer had the croup. He had taken on the permanent position of driver of the coach when Bruno Smith left for California. Ivan was already an experienced driver from the Great Lakes area, learning to drive a stage on the Chicago run before the war. He had come west after the war like so many former solders. He was tall and large-boned with dark hair and beard, and about ten years older than Joe. During the time that he had driven the stage, Joe had found him quiet, reliable and loyal to the stage line. On a few occasions they had discussed the war, Ivan having fought for the Union at Gettysburg, where Joe's brother James had died and was buried. Ivan had been present when President Lincoln had made his speech at the burial grounds, and Joe had listened to the man's recollections, before they had mutually agreed to put aside the war years and were now friends.

The shotgun messenger and relief driver, housed permanently at the station, was named Hank Philips, a recent comer from Pennsylvania hired by Wallace Tisdale, the Western Division Agent. He was a jolly, rotund fellow, quick to make jokes of the many passengers who rode the stage. Several times, Joe had reprimanded him for it, but he couldn't seem to stop the practice. Joe had learned to ignore it, as long as his jokes were not meant to harm their guests. Not yet twenty, Hank was too young to know the tragedy of the war, and Joe sometimes saw in him an echo of his friend Jeremiah. He had admitted that he ran away from home to escape an abusive stepfather. He had also learned his trade on the Chicago to Philadelphia run. The men often sat and discussed the horses and route in the East.

Joe opened the door to the bunkhouse, and walked to Slim's door and knocked, but received no answer. He knocked again and assumed the animal handler must be in the barn with a sick animal. With his sharp eye for detail, he noticed someone had carelessly thrown a harness on the floor in the hallway instead of hanging it neatly in its place on a peg. He picked it up and examined it closely. He saw a small puncture, and the worn leather sides were split. He hung it up, a frown on his face. He retraced his steps and crossed to the shed that housed the goats.

"Slim, you in here?" He paused a moment.

"Yes, Joe, I'll be with you as soon as I finish milking Lolita. She's being cranky today. While you wait, will you look at Prissy? She doesn't seem to be carrying this foal well. I'm worried about her." His voice was muffled by his close contact with the hide of the nanny goat.

"Prissy? Do you think she'll lose the foal? I have great hopes for it. Tisdale was pleased to think she might become part of a new bloodline when he last came for a visit." Joe frowned, as he thought of the horse that had been named for the woman who had accompanied his parents from Indiana to the station. Priscilla St. John was a huge woman, nearly six feet tall, arrogant and short-tempered; she had been sent as a spy to test him by her brother, Willard Jameson, who worked for the Wells Fargo Stage Line. Joe had turned down the chance to live in Denver in a fine house, and sit at a desk instead of the hard physical labor of a station manager. He brought his attention back to Slim.

"I don't know. She doesn't seem to be strong; she's not eating and nips at me when I examine her." Slim came from the interior of the goat shed with a bucket of warm milk in his hand. He went to a shelf of clean cloths, and lifting one from the pile, covered the bucket. There was only one nanny now, the other having tripped on a pool of ice and broken her leg. Slim had been forced to put her down.

With Slim still carrying the bucket, the two men left the shed and crossed to the barn. Joe opened the heavy double doors, and reached for the lantern. It was always dark in the barn, since there were no windows. He left the front door open to help light the room and lit the wick. A soft glow came from the new source of light, and they walked down the aisle to the mare's stall. Holding the lantern high, Joe gave out a groan of despair when he opened the stall door. Slim put the bucket down and followed him into the enclosure where the mare was lying on the straw. He gave a sharp exclamation of alarm as the horse raised her head, but her eyes were dull, and he knew she was weak and clearly in labor.

Forgetting the milk in the bucket, the two men worked frantically to save the mare, but within moments after giving birth to a filly, she gave a weak neigh and died. Joe felt a clinch of pain in his gut, for the mare had been his own, given to him by MacGregor who had brought the supply train through in the first year of his position as manager. Slim was busy with the foal, and Joe stood by helplessly. He heard someone at the barn door, and turning from Slim and the horses, he started to leave.

"Leave some of the milk, Joe; I'll need it to feed the filly. If Peter is up, send him here; I can use his help."

"Right. Thanks, Slim, I know you have things to do here. I'll send Papa and get the horses ready for the westbound stage; and the mules ready for Rusty if he decides not to stay the night. I'm sorry about Prissy. She was a good horse." Joe found a second bucket, cleaned it with a cloth, and poured some of the milk into it. He turned but was stopped by Slim's voice.

"Damn, Joe." Slim paused, letting a heavy sigh escape into the air. He pressed at one eye with his finger. "I know what the mare meant to you, and I wish we could have done more. I loved her, too. I'll do what I can to save the filly, but I don't have any fine expectations. Wish I had another new mother to nurse her. I'll try the milk and see if she'll accept it."

Joe could hear the grief in the animal handler's reply and turned with the milk bucket in his hand, in time to almost bump into Ivan.

"What's going on? When you didn't come to the corral, I decided to come see where you are." He took in the scene in the stall and knew why Joe had been delayed. He sighed. "Prissy? That's a shame. Will the foal live?" Ivan wasn't an experienced horseman, but he could see the distress on the other men's faces.

"We don't know if she'll take the milk without her mother. Come on, I need to tell my father, and we have to get the horses and mules ready for the coaches." With one last glance at the fallen mare and the wobbling filly trying to stand for the first time, Joe left the barn, his face pale and his eyes sad.

Coming from the house were his father and Standing Tree, smoke encircling their heads as they walked. Hank paced himself a few steps behind them. Joe increased his speed, leaving Ivan in his wake. Once again he noticed the Indian limping.

"Papa." He called to his father who had turned toward the corrals.

"Yes, son?" Peter waited for Joe and the stage driver to reach them.

"Papa, Prissy's given birth to a fine filly, but I'm afraid we lost the mother. Slim needs your help with the youngster. He's going to try to feed her some of the goat's milk, but he isn't certain she'll survive; she's so weak and feeble."

"Damnation. I'm sorry, son. She was a good mare. I'll help

43

Slim. When you select the animals for the coaches, we'll haul Prissy to the forest and bury her. Eat your meal and go on with your day; we'll take care of the other matters." Leaving Joe with the two coachmen, Peter strolled briskly to the barn.

Standing Tree sat down under his favorite tree to enjoy his smoke, his eyes following the actions of the men. Joe said nothing as he led the men to the corrals. His thoughts were in turmoil, but he noticed the fog was lifting as he opened the gate to the mule corral. He walked among the animals and selected six to pull the stage back to the Mozier station. Ivan stayed with the mules, examining them carefully while Joe and Hank selected six horses for the black coach. Each of the coaches, although running on a regular schedule each week, didn't make the run if there were no passengers. Joe never knew how many passengers to expect on the weekly runs.

He and Hank hitched the team, and Hank drove the coach out of its shelter, unhitched the horses, and led them to the holding corral and gave them some grain in the trough. He made sure there was water in the tank, while Joe examined the coach, especially the loose front wheel. He decided it needed to be changed and went to the barn to fetch a spare. He rolled it out to the coach and went for his tool box. Hank had disappeared, and Joe saw him talking to Standing Tree. There had been some friction when the young man had first arrived, but he'd come to accept the Indian as one of the members of Joe's family.

The latest supply wagons had brought him two new wheels, made by the finest wheelwrights in Denver. The supplies no longer came from St. Louis, and Joe missed the chance to speak with men bringing news of Ned Baldwin. He received letters from him occasionally and knew the family in Davidson County was well. Matthew had finished his schooling and was driving a coach for a local firm in order to gain the experience necessary for the long routes. The fashion-conscious Gladys had been sent to a girl's finishing school in Boston and married before the term had ended. She was happy with the more modern society in which she now lived.

Calling to Hank and Ivan to come help him, they soon had the new wheel on the stage and inspected the vehicle for other flaws. Ivan dusted the interior and pulled out the dope pot to sludge the axles. Hank went to the bunkhouse and came back with his hand satchel and threw it into the front boot. Having done all he could until the stage arrived from the Mozier station, Joe went into the barn to check on the filly. He found Slim and Peter with one of the other mares, talking.

"What do you think? Will the filly live?" He looked around.

"Yes, I think so. She took the milk from my hand, and I have the rubber-nippled bottle handy for later. Come see." Slim led the way to the stall where Prissy still lay, stiff and silent. The filly was standing on her feet, sniffing at her dead mother.

"Shouldn't you put her in one of the other stalls?" Joe spoke over the lump in his throat. His head ached with this morning's chores. He felt nauseous at the aroma in the stall.

"I will. I was checking on Samantha. She's due, too. I'd hate to lose two mares at the same time." Samantha was one of the more recent acquisitions at the station, having been brought in during the hunt for more mustangs. Instead of training her as a draft horse, Joe had put her in with Mack, his stallion.

The paint colt from his first attempt at gathering the feral horses had long since left the station with a herd of draft animals for the stage line. Joe only kept a few saddle horses and enough stage stock for the once-a-week route. There were ten mules used for the Mozier route; the rest of the animals were for breeding or too young for service. He'd never thought of himself as a horse trainer, but that's what he'd become, with the help of his father and Slim. Joe, Slim and Standing Tree had gone on a mustang hunt last summer, and he'd taken the untrained horses on to Mozier Station to replenish their older stock. He still kept three donkeys for breeding.

Gathering strong ropes and a mule, they dragged the mare out of the stall and into the forest where they took turns digging a pit for her. Joe dumped some lime in the hole to help decomposition and left after filling in the pit. There was no farewell service; they had no time for sentimentality.

Four

Hannah was stirring the pot of beans, while Ruth was watching Fuller as he ran through the Public Room on his short, stubby legs. He hadn't yet lost his baby fat, and spoke only a few choice words. His hair was dark, his eyes gray. Her heart had rejoiced when he said "mama" the first time. He used the word for both women, not able to understand the relationship. But, his papa he knew; for the tall man cuddled him and swung him into the air with care and strong arms. Fuller would laugh and scream with pleasure. His grandfather was more calm and restful, taking him into his lap or reading to him from a book.

The other members of the household he accepted as belonging to him. Ivan seldom held him or played games, but Slim took delight in teaching him things that little boys needed to know. Hank ignored him most of the time; complaining of his noise and running feet. But, in a special way, not understood by the others, it was Standing Tree to whom Fuller ran when he was upset. The Indian would take him in his arms and wrap his blanket around him until his tears stopped and he was at peace. At such time, either Hannah or Ruth would lift him from the

Indian's lap and distract him until his sunny nature appeared again.

The smell of freshly baked bread permeated the room, and was joined by the tart aroma of spice and apple pie baking in the second oven. Joe took a deep breath as he entered the room. From the activity, he knew the women were preparing for the onslaught of passengers for the day and night.

"Hello, darling. I have sad news. The mare Prissy died while giving birth to a filly. We've buried her in the forest a far distance from the spring." He kissed his wife on the cheek and gave his mother a smile. He lifted the pail of milk onto the table.

"Oh, Joe. I'm so sorry. I know you'll miss her. She was your first start on the herd of horses. What will you name the filly?" Hannah was wearing a pink calico dress and a large white apron, with her hair twisted on top of her head. The women of the station didn't wear the large crinoline undergarments of current fashion, but plain skirts, easier to care for and move in around the room. Hannah had a pair of soft moccasins on her feet, and her belly was full with her second child. She hoped it was a girl for she wished for a precious daughter to dress and brush her hair.

"We haven't chosen a name. I don't know yet whether she'll survive. Slim will take care of her. He kept part of the milk for the animal." He gave her a mournful look, and she laughed.

"It's not the first time," she said. "Would you like some coffee?"

"Yes, thank you. That will go well. I have a few minutes to spare." He sat in his place at the head of the large table. He looked with pride at his son, now sitting among his toys in front of the fireplace. "Mama, are you sure you want another boy to cause you grief?" It was a joke because he knew of Hannah's desire for a girl and liked to tease her. If the truth were known, he'd like a girl himself.

Hannah brought a cup and filled it with the hot, dark brown liquid. She gave him an exasperated smile and poked him gently on the arm. He looked at her and grinned. Ruth left them alone and went to sit in the rocking chair while she watched Fuller play.

Joe took a sip of the coffee and said, "Sit with me a minute." Hannah placed the pot on the stove to keep it warm but not boiling. She sighed and sat.

He glanced at his wife's scarred face and remembered when he and his brothers were young boys. His older brothers had teased him because he had sought out Hannah to talk with while walking home from church. He thought her beautiful, although most people would find her unattractive. Two years older than him, she had an inner spirit and gracious manner for those who would abuse her.

"I was thinking this morning of the first days we came to Sweetwater. Do you remember the way it was, with Taylor and the building crew, and Jackson's men felling the logs to build the road? It seems hard to believe there was no road through the forest to Denver." He sighed and took her hand gently in his own large, calloused one.

"Yes, I remember. You told the men that I baked the best pies in Indiana, and I felt overwhelmed with the whole thing. I was so tired after the trip in the stage, and the thought of the responsibility of feeding them frightened me. And, when Buck Jones came in that Conestoga, I wanted to go back to Indiana." She looked over at her son and mother-in-law. Ruth was listening but pretending to be thinking of something else.

"But, you never told me this. I felt guilty going off and

49

leaving you, but I had to know about the box canyon and the mustangs."

She smiled with her whole face, and Joe's heart beat faster. "And, it's paid us well, for now I have my own sewing machine and meat grinder. Now, leave us to get on with our chores; the passengers will be here soon, and I have a lot of work to do." She kissed him on the lips and shooed him away. He walked across the room, picked up his son, lifted him high in the air and Fuller squealed with joy. Named James Fuller Hadley, for the man who had died to save Joe's life when Dakota came at him with a gun, he was born in the first year at the station.

"Papa, Papa," he said and fell into the strong arms of his father. Joe gave him a hug and looked up to see a twinkle in his mother's eyes. Slightly embarrassed, he gave her the boy and walked out of the room, his face as red as an apple.

He paused on the step to look at the gold-plated timepiece in his pocket, also bought with the bonus money earned from the breeding of the mustangs with his station stock. It lacked two hours of time for Rusty to appear, if the stage came through. He crossed to the bunkhouse, took the tools from the supply room and began to make repairs on the harness he had found on the floor. It was something he often did when troubled or tired, to calm his mind. The harnesses had to be checked after every trip and repaired periodically. He felt it another of his responsibilities of running the station, along with caring for the needs of the animals, although most of that was left to his animal handler.

As his eyes and hands were engaged in his work, his mind kept up a steady stream of memories. He remembered the first time he and Hannah had stopped at the Mozier station, and he heard Sam Mozier warn him against the Indians stealing the horses. A grin crossed his face, thinking of his idea to brand the horses. The new horses and mules were branded in the spring with the mark of the stage line. Only Mack now carried his own brand, a rocking H. Sam had wandered off during that first hard winter and frozen to death. Rebecca and the children had taken the stage to Denver, and she had married a merchant in town. They received a letter from her occasionally telling the news of the family.

The animal handler, Tim, had managed the station and cared for the animals, with the assistance of Rusty, Grover and the other stage drivers on the north-south route, but since he wasn't married, a new attendant named Charles Youngblood and his wife Irma were sent to the station. Irma, with her two boys, Jasper and George, had come a few times to visit with Hannah and Ruth, while on their way to Denver for shopping and pleasure. She was a jolly, motherly sort, and her children well-behaved. They stayed overnight before completing the trip, and again stayed on the way east to Mozier Station.

Soon after his arrival, Youngblood and Tim had an argument, and Tim left the station and moved out of the Territory. Enoch Barclay came as the new animal handler, a capable middle-aged man from Maryland.

Joe was the only one left of the original station managers; Emily Blessing had left her husband after a brawl in his saloon at Buckboard left two dead and several injured patrons. She'd returned to her beloved New Hampshire and lived with an aunt. They hadn't heard from her since her arrival in the East. Obediah was released from service, and the rumors indicated he'd gone to California. He was replaced by Shadrach Weaver and his wife Bessie. Tisdale had allowed the saloon to remain a part of the station, but Shad was a more mature, sensible man and kept a tight control over the drinking and gambling. They had no children.

At Rockland Station within a few months, Usamah Jones was found to be lazy and irresponsible, leaving all the work to his black servants, who ran off one dark night in the wagon with two of the station's horses. Tisdale had ruled it a just payment for their forced labor and had replaced him with a man named Moore and his wife Jane. Joe hadn't met him until his recent trip to Denver, but had heard through the passengers who came through on the stage that he was a good attendant and responsible manager. The animal handler, Hatton, was still there.

Joe realized that he had been sitting for a long time. He hung up the repaired harness and took out his timepiece. He frowned as he looked at the face. It was almost time for the stage to arrive. He put away his tools, and strolled out of the room and into the afternoon sun. Everything was quiet, as he looked around the yard. He gazed at the mountains and walked over to Standing Tree sitting under his tree.

"The coach will be here soon. Many people, food for all. What's wrong with your leg?" He pointed at the Indian's leg. "Pain? Open wound?" He wasn't sure the man understood him, although he had learned several words in the Arapahoe language, and the Indian understood many English words. He wore the same type shirt and trousers as the other men, with his constant blanket wrapped around his shoulders in both hot and cold weather. He carried a knife in a scabbard on his hip; and a deer skin bag covered with tiny beads on a length of rawhide around his neck.

"Much pain. Make scratch on leg. Put poultice of damp earth on it. No worry, Yo Hadley."

Joe frowned and noticed the man's face was flushed, but he had no more time to question him, for coming up the road from the creek was the sound of mules' hooves, and suddenly the loud, melodious sound of a trumpet could be heard. The stage had arrived.

Joe turned and glanced around the station grounds. Slim and Peter came from the barn. Ivan strolled from the corrals, and Hank closed the door of the outhouse and headed toward them. Rusty stopped the coach in front of the station door with a curse of indignation as the mules breathed heavily in the dust raised by their hooves. Joe called out, "Hey, Rusty, glad to see you made it; hello, Grover, any trouble on the line?"

Rusty set the brake and settled himself on the box. Grover climbed down and stood by silently. With half his mind, Joe noticed that the guard wasn't happy. He tensed as he opened the door.

Out came a woman dressed in the fashion of the times, in a dark maroon dress, decorated with white, and a black hat perched on her head. She was followed by a young, slender woman dressed in yellow. As they were adjusting to the stoppage of motion of the coach; Joe heard a curse, and a burly man of average height, with a beard and long side hairs, stepped down, spouting vile language and red-faced. He wore spectacles and a tall silk hat, and was dressed in a dark suit and white shirt. Following him was a lean, blond-haired man clutching a leather satchel and cane. The older man turned and grabbed the cane from the hand of the younger, and Joe was quick to see that another man was stepping down, a miner from his looks, dressed in a blue plaid shirt, corduroy trousers and brown boots.

Joe turned to the ladies, "Welcome to Sweetwater Station.

Please come into the house out of the sun; my wife and mother are ready to welcome you. Sirs, you are welcome. Have you had a pleasant journey?" He was trying his best not to lose his temper; for it was unseemly for the behavior of the man in front of ladies. Out of the corner of his eye, he saw Slim and Peter go to the head of the mules and calm them. Peter started to unhitch the team. Standing Tree stood silently under the tree. Ivan and Hank remained in place, staring at the strangers. Joe shut the door of the coach and turned to see Hannah come from the house with a smile of welcome.

"Good day, Ladies. Welcome to Sweetwater; please come in and have a cup of refreshing tea." She guided them up the steps and held the door for them to move inside. The heavy-set man turned to Joe and looked him up and down as if assessing his character. Joe smiled, putting his most charming self on display, but the man turned from him and started castigating the younger man by his side. Thinking it was none of his business, Joe turned toward Rusty, just dropping from his place on the box. He gave him a questioning look, and they moved out of hearing range of the pompous, arrogant windbag, for that's what Joe thought him.

"What's going on, Rusty? Who is that man?" He glanced at Grover who headed with an angry shuffle toward the outhouse. Ivan and Hank retreated to the bunkhouse. Joe saw them talking as they entered through the door. He had meant to ask about the harness dropped on the floor, but it suddenly didn't seem important.

"Calls himself Colonel Appleby; says he was a colonel in the late war, but I don't recall hearing of such a man. A politician from Washington, I heard him tell the miner. Poor secretary is named Trindle; didn't hear his front handle. The older lady is his wife and the younger his daughter. Didn't catch their names. Doesn't matter; I'm glad to get shed of them. They been nothing but trouble since they climbed aboard the stage. Even Irma at Mozier didn't know what to do about the situation. Me and Grover ain't staying. We'll eat and run; can't take no more of the windbag's voice." He took a cigar from the tin in his pocket and lighted it. He waved at Slim, calling out, "Ain't staying, Slim. Hitch the mules and give these a good rubbing down, they've earned it." Slim nodded and looked to Joe for instructions.

"It's alright, Slim. I'll see to Hannah and Mama and meet you at the corral." Slim led the mules to the water trough and Peter went into the house. Joe waited until Grover came from the outhouse. He looked closely at the coach, noticing the dusty wheels, the overall appearance, then walked to the rear boot and began to empty it of luggage. Grover came to help him. He'd left his shotgun on the seat of the coach, since they weren't spending the night. He didn't speak for a few minutes.

"I don't envy you the task of corralling those strangers tonight. That man is a menace and a coward. Only a coward would speak like he does to his secretary and wife and daughter. If I had to hang around him much longer, I'd have to give him a punch in the gut and smash his face. It was all I could do to keep quiet until now. Rusty and I agreed not to stay. If we get tired, we'll pull over and sleep on the ground. Better to go back to Mozier than cause Hannah and Ruth embarrassment. You watch out for him, Joe. He's the type that's dangerous. Not with a gun or knife but with his words and manner." He helped Joe move the baggage to the porch.

"They're staying the night then? I could have Ivan drive them on to Buckboard, if you think he's out to make trouble.

The coach is ready and the horses fresh. Who's the other fellow? The one in the blue shirt." Joe turned to look at the grounds of the station and saw Slim bringing out the mules for the return trip. He wanted to avoid trouble and go to him, but he had to protect his womenfolk.

"Yes, he paid for the extra night. Said it was for the benefit of the ladies, who are tired from the long trip. Came from the steamboat on the Arkansas, so they need a night's rest after two days riding coach. The other fellow calls himself Dick Othman. Looks like a miner, the way he's dressed. You watch him; there's no way of knowing if he's a bad character. I'm going to get some grub." He took a step forward.

Joe called to the man's back, "We lost the mare this morning. The one called Prissy; she gave us a fine filly before she died, that being if Slim can keep her alive."

"Sorry to hear 'bout that," Grover called over his shoulder, but he made no further indications of sympathy.

Joe picked up the man's valise and one of the carpetbags, and Grover opened the door. As far as his job was concerned, Joe supposed, Grover was finished for this trip. He wasn't responsible after the luggage was removed from the stage coach. But, he picked up a carpetbag and went inside, and Joe was grateful for that.

Five

The others hadn't waited for Joe. He left the valise and carpetbag beside the one dropped by Grover at the front door, and went back for the rest of the luggage. He noticed there was more than was allowed by the stage company. The passengers were allowed only one piece of luggage and it was supposed to weigh less than thirty pounds, but the colonel's party had two extra pieces. He didn't figure it was his business, so he stepped inside the house.

"It seems we have quite a crowd." He whispered his words to his wife, as he stood behind her, overlooking the pot she stirred at the stove. "Have they caused you any difficulties?"

"Oh, Joe," she replied, pulling a loose strand of hair from her cheek and giving him a quick kiss on his face, "I'm just hoping we have enough food. I always try to prepare plenty, but I never expected this number of passengers to disembark all at once."

"You'll do fine, and it smells delicious." He saw her flushed look, but he also knew this wasn't her first meal to serve to the stage company's clientele, and she'd seen them rant and rave—

and stood up to a few. He had a good wife who knew how to handle herself in a difficult situation. He chuckled at the memory of her with a gun and standing on the porch to ward off an irritated stage hand.

"You find this amusing?" Hannah clattered her stirring utensil against the side of the iron pot and covered it with a lid.

"I find you wonderful. I think I'll head to my seat at this time."

"You better, before I send you there myself." She nudged him with her elbow, but there was more of an intimate moment there than that of irritation.

Joe ducked his head in embarrassment and went to the table and sat down in his regular place as head of the family. He noticed that Standing Tree didn't come in and was worried about him. With all the excitement of the arrival, he'd been interrupted in his talk about the man's leg. He thought to ask Peter, but his father was off to the other side of the goings-on, and he decided to bring up the matter at a later time.

He glanced at Ruth, but she seemed her usual calm self as she served the food and drinks. The boy, Fuller, sat in his chair, and Joe teased with him for a moment, asking him if he thought his mother's food was good.

"Like it." Fuller knocked his spoon against the table, leaving a spot of food. The miner Dick Othman sat next to him and shied away each time the boy waved his utensil in the air, but Joe thought nothing of it. It was no different than the way his son ate at every meal.

"Sir, if you would be so good as to watch your child, I would appreciate it." Othman finally spoke, although he didn't press the matter.

Joe saw why, when Ivan leaned into the man and growled

something unintelligible to Joe, and Othman immediately went silent, giving Joe furtive glances. Through it all, Fuller ate a good meal, although some of it covered his face and shirt front. Hannah poured Joe a cup of coffee and he took a sip, but she didn't linger. From the stiff way she walked, he could tell she was upset or angry. Probably at the man's treatment of Fuller. Peter seemed poised to protect the womenfolk, so Joe knew his family was in good hands, and he filled his plate and began to eat. There was venison stew, with potatoes, onions, carrots and cabbage, sliced tomatoes, and sour pickles from the cucumbers grown in their own garden. There was fresh bread, and a peach cobbler, and johnnycakes for desert.

Even as he filled his gullet, the colonel had begun pontificating, both loudly and with great emphasis, talking of the recent actions of the United States Congress concerning the voting rights of the black men. They had passed a bill and sent it to the states to be ratified. There was talk whether Georgia would sign the oath to rejoin the Union of states. Without their consent, the colonel said, the matter would not be settled.

Joe glanced at the man called Trindle and imagined he saw fear in his eyes. The miner kept his eyes on his plate, but his cheeks were pink from resentment or exasperation.

In response to the colonel's opinionated statements, Joe stepped into the one-sided conversation, in an attempt to shift the topic of discussion.

"Colonel, have you heard of this new game of baseball?"

"Why," the colonel blustered, as if Joe were trying to undermine his train of thought, "do you doubt my knowledge of the modern world?"

"I'm just curious if you know anyone who has ever played. It seems a most unusual sport for men to be chasing each other over a simple ball." He smiled warmly, hoping to get the man to follow his lead. By the look on the colonel's face, he suspected his choice of conversation might be making matters worse.

"My youth is over, my good man. I look forward in my views, for looking backwards does nothing except create further dissention between the youth that want no more than to fritter their time away, and those of us who ponder over greater ideas and grander issues. I think you'd do better to dwell along the same line."

The colonel's wife, Colleen, placed a hand on his arm and murmured, "We all believe in you, my dear." Her eyes were down, as if the statement were one she repeated often, and without real conviction. She continued, gazing around the table at the other passengers, "I look forward to living in the city. Tell me, Mr. Hadley, have you and your wife attended the opera? I understand a new Italian comedy has been introduced at the Denver Theater for the general public."

Before Joe could answer in the affirmative, the colonel cleared his throat gruffly, and he returned to his pontification about voting rights and black men.

After several moments of the continued bigotry, Joe tried once again to change the subject of conversation, but was drowned out by the booming voice of the politician, who refused to let him speak. Finally, Rusty and Grover rose and with a word of regret to Hannah and Ruth, they left the room, to prepare for their journey.

Ivan and Hank followed, and the atmosphere seemed to change, since the man no longer had a captive audience. Trindle and the miner left, after Joe told them they would be given a room in the bunkhouse. Joe thought he heard a sigh of relief from both men, but it might have been the scraping of the chair against wood as the colonel rose from his seat. Joe impulsively rose with him, and with the pretext of showing him his room for the night, allowed the other men, except Peter, to escape. He knew his father would stay with the women while they finished their chores.

Joe asked the colonel which of the bags were his and his wife's and took them to the bedroom; he pointed out the facilities in the backyard and shut the door behind the man, hoping he would stay in the room for a while. He was frustrated, however, by the man's joining him as he left the house after whispering to Hannah, asking if she was comfortable. She nodded her head and smiled.

When he noticed the colonel had followed him outside, he turned to him and started to speak. "We had a little excitement this morning, sir. One of my best mares died while giving birth to a filly. Are you interested in fine horseflesh? I didn't start out to breed horses, but I have some excellent animals, if you would like to see them."

"I have owned an animal or two." The colonel huffed a bit, although his statement was very obtuse. "I perhaps could give you some advice, if you wish to listen to it."

Joe nodded and continued as he walked to the stage in which the man had just traveled. "If you'll give me a few minutes to get this coach on its way back east, I'll show you a few of my stock."

Without giving him a chance to object or leave, and quite irritated by the man's presumptive pandering, Joe took the dope pot from under the back of the stage and began to examine the axles, explaining the use of the grease and the danger of the wheels being dry in the desert sand. Replacing the pot to its place, he then went to the mules and looked at their teeth, their hooves, their ears, and manes and tails. He caught a glimpse of Rusty and Grover, and was certain they knew what he was doing, distracting the man until they were ready to leave. Joe introduced Slim as his veterinarian and animal handler, pointed out the distant mountains and the clear high plains air; the spring and the flowing creek. At last, he gave a sign with his hand that the men would recognize and led the colonel to the barn; pointing out the shelter for the coach, the bunkhouse and the sheds.

As soon as Joe was inside the barn, Rusty climbed into the box. Grover mounted his seat and they drove away with a toot of the bugle and a cloud of dust. Joe heard the faint sound from inside the barn, and led Appleby to one of the stalls containing a large, fine animal.

"This is Modred, one of my best. He's a mix of flesh, from a fine animal back East mixed with wild stock we captured not far from here. I feel the mix of well-bred Eastern stock and the hearty attributes of the local animals have created the finest piece of flesh possible. Do you agree?" Joe looked away and fought a smile. He could pontificate as well as Appleby, if he chose to do so. Stepping back and allowing the man into the stall, he gave him time to examine Modred's virtues, and led him to the stall of Tennessee, whom he had named after the place where his friend Jeremiah had been born. The stallion gave a whinny of welcome, for Joe had raised him and trained him as a saddle horse from his birth, shunning the thought of making him into a draft horse for the stage line.

"Ah, now this is a piece of horseflesh!" The colonel remarked on Tennessee's fine form, ignoring Joe having extolled the virtues of Modred, as if only Appleby could evaluate true quality in the animals accurately. "This is truly a fine creature. Tell me of him."

Joe proceeded to describe how he was bred of Mack and a mustang mare, and that he, too, found him to be a magnificent animal, one of the first of his string of horses to be bred on the station grounds. He moved from Tennessee to Eva, shifting the colonel away from the stallion to his favorite mare, who had produced two colts for him.

Eventually, the colonel seemed to mellow, remarking that he was pleasantly surprised at the quality and stability of the relay station. He was in a gentler mood as he smoked and sat with the men after the evening meal. Joe was not surprised that the secretary spent the night in the bunkhouse, without the harassment of his employer.

The next morning, before sunrise, Joe, Peter, Slim and the coachmen were preparing for the journey to Buckboard. With Ivan in the box and Hank seated beside him, his shotgun in the crook of his arm, the black coach left the station with the colonel and his retinue, and the inhabitants of Sweetwater Station breathed a collective sigh of relief. It was only later that Joe had a chance to discuss with Hannah the affairs of the ladies.

"The colonel and I had a time of it last evening. Only when I discussed horses with him did he warm to me. I was certain that my confrontation at the meal would set him against me for all time."

"I was so glad you kept him away from the womenfolk. They finally chose to talk, and they shared some of how they've suffered because of the man's ill treatment of them." Hannah's face was hard, telling of her anger at the revelation.

"I'm not surprised, though I regret hearing it. It fit with the

63

man. At least they had a few moments during the evening to spend time with my good wife. I'm sure it lifted their spirits somewhat." He smiled and kissed her on the cheek, and was relieved to see the tension in her face relax.

It was good that he hadn't heard of the abuse before, because he agreed with Grover, that it would have been hard for him to control his anger at the man. To think such a bully was hoping to be governor of the Territory made him cringe with despair. He'd met the present governor, and he was a fine man. He shrugged it away, telling himself it wasn't his business and went to find Standing Tree.

The Indian was lying in his blanket under the tree, raging with fever. Joe went for Slim, calling to him, "Man, have you had a look at Standing Tree this morning?"

"I saw him, sure, asleep in his usual spot. He was limping yesterday, but he's worse today?" Slim didn't seem particularly aggrieved at Joe's question.

"His skin's hot as sun-baked bricks. Come see if you can help him." Together they strode towards the old Indian's regular resting spot.

"This man is seriously ill." Slim pressed his hand against his face and found it covered with perspiration. "Help me move him inside."

The men helped him into the house and placed him on the bed in one of the bedrooms, where Slim cut away his trousers' leg.

"My word, Joe, what was the man thinking?" There was the matted mess of roots and soil that Standing Tree had used to heal himself. "Did you know about this, Joe?"

"I did. I hadn't seen it, however, and I assumed it was an old Indian remedy. I had no idea the wound was festered and swollen."

"I minister to animals, but it doesn't take a people doctor to see this injury is serious." He cursed under his breath, muttering that he might be too late to save the leg.

Joe cursed louder because he had sensed something was wrong but had allowed the cares of the animals and the passengers to override his concern for his friend.

"Hannah," Joe called. "We need your help with Standing Tree."

"When I saw you bring him in, I knew it must be serious. I have water heating already." She stepped into the room and blanched. "Oh, Joe, this is worse than anything I pictured. I'll prepare bandages for the wound."

Hannah brought hot water and a stack of clean cloths. Ruth stood by with a lantern, while Slim tried his salves and medicines on the wound.

"Standing Tree, you must drink some of this." Slim held the man's head up, and he tipped some laudanum past his lips, nodding at Joe and smiling when the man seemed to swallow it down. He took thumb forceps and gently drew a thorn from under the skin of the leg, then bathed the wound with an evil-smelling substance from a brown bottle. He placed the cork back in the bottle and set it on the table. Releasing him to lie prone, Slim changed positions and bandaged the leg with clean cloths. When he finished, he took the pan of still-warm water and the dirtied cloths back to Hannah, thanking her for being such an excellent help, and assuring both her and Joe that he would keep a regular watch on the man if some of the other men could take care of the outside chores. Joe agreed, knowing that Slim was the closest they had to a doctor.

Joe came in twice to check on his friend. Standing Tree

raged in his own language, and Hannah prayed for him. For two days, the Indian fought the fever and the pain, and at last his eyes turned clear, his skin became cool to the touch and he was able to eat some broth without becoming nauseous. They knew he was on the mend when he called for his pipe and some tobacco. Joe was so grateful, he hadn't the heart to refuse him. He left the room as Standing Tree puffed away in contentment. Joe marched into the forest and sat for a long time on a tree trunk, thinking of the day the Indian had come, alone, lost and hungry to the station. He recalled his anger on the day that Buck Jones and Standing Tree left the station and returned with the wolf skins; of the times they had gone north in search of mustangs and the trips to hunt deer.

He returned from the forest, plunged into work, and when the coach arrived a week later from the east, Joe was his charming, cheerful self again. He seldom thought of the war years and his experiences as a Confederate soldier. He was content to hold his son in his arms at night and read to him from one of the books sent by Ned Baldwin when he had been their division agent. He read the Denver City newspapers which usually were a week late, but welcome to the isolated residents of the station.

He and Hannah rode the horses a few miles into the forest and camped out under the stars, leaving the child in Ruth's care. It would be the last ride until the new child was born, and they enjoyed the time away from the others and the responsibility of the station. She came back stiff and sore but with a smile on her face. She set out her watercolors and started a painting of the creek, recalling the towering mountains embellished with scattered pockets of snow, and the flowers lining the banks alongside the rushing water. It was her favorite memory of the day.

When Rusty and Grover pulled into the station, Joe was waiting under Standing Tree's favorite cottonwood, the Indian beside him. They had been keeping up a strange conversation of half-English, Indian sign language, about the most recent mustang hunt when they had sighted the black stallion again. Although they had come across small herds and were able to capture them, Joe had only twice seen the mighty black stallion with his massive herd of underlings. He estimated maybe twenty-five to thirty horses were in the group. What a catch that would be, if they could find the black. From the way of the creek, he heard the splash of the wheels of the old brown coach and then the loud, melodious sound of the bugle. His heart started beating fast in anticipation, for he never knew how many or what characters might step out of the coach. This time was special.

"Heh, Joe, got someone important this time," Rusty yelled from the box. Joe looked toward Grover, but he just shrugged. When the stage was at a complete stop, without waiting for Rusty, Joe opened the door. A rather large, full-figured woman dressed in blue stepped down; followed by a younger woman with blonde curls and bright eyes. Next, a middle-aged man in dark suit and white shirt came out and marched toward the outhouse, not waiting for the ladies. Joe stepped aside, and started to close the door, thinking that was all the passengers, when a tall, thin young man hesitated, then poked his head out the door, and cautiously stepped down.

His face was familiar, and Joe was certain he knew him, but he was distracted by the commotion when Hannah and Ruth greeted the women.

"Welcome, ladies, come in and I'll shortly have your

dinner on the table." The two ladies were ushered up the steps and into the house.

Joe turned to the young man. When the newcomer raised his hat and the sunlight glowed on his face, his identify was revealed.

"Matthew Baldwin, how good to see you. This is a nice surprise. How is your father, your mother?" Joe smiled his most charming smile. It was Ned Baldwin's son, the young man who had been in school when they had first met in the stage agent's office three years ago, when Joe and Hannah had come fresh from the steamboat on the Arkansas River. Joe looked him up and down; he had filled out, seemed stronger and his face was darker from days in the sun.

"Hello, Mr. Hadley. My parents are well, and so are Gladys, Tom, Sally, Micah, Ruth, Fannie and Ellie." He laughed, "Pa says to tell you he found an old book you might enjoy when you have time to read. It's about King Arthur and the Knights of the Round Table. It's a good book. I read it on the way here." He lifted his hand, and enclosed in it was a thin, brown leather-covered book of poetry. Joe took it from him and quickly flipped through the pages, pleased that Ned had sent it.

"Thank you, Matthew. This is going to take some time to read." By this time, Rusty and Grover had climbed down and were listening to them. Slim was standing at the head of the team, ready to unhitch them and take them to water. Out of the corner of his eye, Joe saw the other man come from the out-house. "Come in, come in; I believe Hannah has dinner almost on the table."

The coachmen stayed with Slim, while Rusty helped unhitch the team. Joe saw Ivan and Hank come out of the bunkhouse to greet their fellow coachmen. Standing Tree started in his slow, shuffling gate to the house. The middle-aged man stopped and stared at him.

"Oh, no," Joe thought to himself. "Trouble."

But, it wasn't the Indian that caused the trouble. It was Hannah's scarred face. Coming in the door after him, Joe didn't see the initial surprise on the man's face. He only heard the Indian's quick defense of Joe's wife. The dog, Jack, was sitting on his haunches, his tail low and still.

"Scarred Woman, my friend. Yo Hadley, my friend. You go." He stood as stiff as a marble statue as he clung to his blanket. Joe knew that it would take only a spark to have the Indian's knife from his scabbard. He gently moved Matthew to the side, and stepped between Standing Tree and the passenger.

"Welcome to Sweetwater Station, sir. I don't believe I caught your name. This is my wife, Hannah, my mother, Ruth, and my friend of the Arapahoe tribe, Standing Tree. Here, let me take your hat and coat. Hannah, how long until we eat?" Joe was filled with indignation at the affront, and he refused to back down. Jack moved to his side, and Joe gave him a pat on the head.

"About an hour, Joe." Hannah responded.

Matthew came from behind Joe and stood next to the table, but it was the man's wife who defused the situation. "How do you do, Mr. Hadley. I'm Grace Willingham, and this is my very rude husband, Ferdinand, and my daughter, Selma. Sit down, Ferdie, and drink a cup of coffee. You'll feel better after you eat. Such a lovely place you have, Mrs. Hadley, with so many trees. I was quite surprised when we crossed the creek to find the lofty pines and spruce." She continued to talk while her husband found a chair and sat down. Ruth poured him a cup of coffee and he took a sip.

69

Standing Tree went to his spot by the fireplace and sat down, but his eyes were alert and watchful, as the man continued to glance his way.

Thinking everything was settled; Joe motioned for Matthew to sit, but he continued to stand. It was then that Hannah recognized him.

"Oh, my. Is it you, Matthew? What a nice surprise. How's your dear mother, and the children?"

Ferdie Willingham looked startled at the attention the young man was receiving from the hosts of the station. He set his cup on the table.

"They're fine, Hannah, and I can see that you have a nice son of your own. Pa told us of the boy." He circled the table and took Fuller into his arms. "Well, well, Fuller, how do you do? I'm Matt Baldwin. I've come a long way to see you." He tickled the boy under the chin, and Fuller laughed at him. "And, is this Jack? My, how he's grown. Hannah, what do you feed him?"

"Oh, just the usual table scraps. Is Gladys happy in her marriage?" Hannah poured Matthew and Joe a cup of coffee while everyone watched as the young man sat down with Fuller still in his arms. The conversation became more general, with even Willingham taking part, his manner changing as the food was soon brought to the table.

Joe turned as Peter came in, followed by Rusty, Grover, Ivan and Hank. Standing Tree came to take his place beside Joe, and Grace Willingham gave her husband a baleful glare, but he said nothing. They all found places at the table, and Joe introduced Matthew Baldwin to the group. When he mentioned he was the son of the stage line's Eastern Agent, Willingham saw him with a new respect in his eyes. The young lady, Selma, preened and glanced at him with soulful eyes. About midway through the meal, Hannah took Fuller and put him back in his chair and began to feed him from a spoon.

When Joe finished eating he rose and started to leave, but was surprised by Willingham. He coughed to clear his throat, and said, "I apologize for my rude behavior. I can only blame it on the long ride we've had through the plains. I'm a newspaper man by trade, and we're going to Denver. I wonder, Mr. Hadley, if I might have some of your time later to discuss the coming of the railroad to the city. Do you think it'll lead to the demise of the long-distance stage lines? I'm sure the readers would be interested in your opinion." He glanced at his wife, who smiled.

"I'd be glad to sit with you this evening when it's cooler, but my men and I have work to do now, if you'll excuse us." He scratched his head, and winked at Hannah. "I'm afraid my opinion isn't worth much, but I would like to know how the northern rail traffic is progressing toward Utah." Joe smiled his most charming smile and turned to get his hat from the peg by the door.

He was followed by the rest of the men, and Willingham was left alone with the ladies and the child, Fuller. He quickly rose and went out the door.

*****

There was no more controversy as Joe and the coachmen and Slim prepared the coach for its trek back to Mozier. Willingham stood beside the barn wall and watched, a pad and pencil in his hand. The men paid him no heed. Joe made his usual inspection of the coach and the mules; Rusty checked the axles himself; Grover talked with Hank, his shotgun hoisted

71

over his left shoulder. Matthew was engaged in conversation with Ivan, while Peter helped Slim in the corral with the horses.

With a toot of his horn, and a loud curse from Grover, Rusty put the mules into motion, and the coach rolled toward the shallow ford of the creek. Joe then had time to walk with Matthew toward the spring where they sat under a giant pine tree and talked about Ned and his family, and the new book he had brought.

Willingham went into the house, and Joe was disturbed to see him go, as he was worried about Hannah and Ruth. He hoped they didn't say anything to the newspaper man that would appear in print. But, he knew he shouldn't worry, for his wife had a grasp of the situation. If possible, she'd send the man into the bedroom assigned to him and give him the option of napping through the afternoon, while offering his wife, Grace, the chance to help the ladies with kitchen chores.

Joe was also certain the daughter Selma would do little more than sulk in a corner chair, perhaps pretending to read a book. He knew Fuller would never be allowed to be such a disagreeable child.

Standing Tree napped under his cottonwood tree, his blanket wrapped tightly around his frail body. Near sunset, he was awakened by the sound of horses' hooves, and Paul Ward drove into the yard from the south. Again, there was excitement and activity as the horses were changed and the guests welcomed. Fortunately, it was four single men, and they were settled into rooms in the bunkhouse, where they were entertained by Ivan, Hank and Slim in a lively game of poker. Paul and Manning didn't stay as they could see Joe had a full house. As soon as the horses were hitched and the coach dusted off, they took off with a bag of johnnycakes and canteens of water in their satchels.

The moon came up large and bright, and the last lingering rays of the sun filtered through the branches of the trees; and Joe sat with Willingham for the promised talk about stage coaches and railroads. Peter and Slim joined in the conversation, and Joe saw the frown on Slim's face as the Easterner told of the progress of the Union Pacific and the politicians in Washington. Matthew sat quietly, smoking a cigar, the dog Jack lying beside him with his brown eyes alert. Joe suspected Matthew knew more than he was saying. His father was a very important man in the running of the stage company. He had told Joe earlier that he was on his way to Denver, to accept a new assignment on the far western border of the Territory.

"You'll miss your family," Joe had told him.

"Joe, I already miss them. The noise and the barking dogs and the street lights, the riverboats chugging with their paddles throwing up water into the air. But, a man has to make his own way in the world. My father is a powerful man; I can't ride on his coattails all my life. He and Mama understand. When Gladys left, Mama cried all night. I'll miss seeing the young ones grow up, but it's time for me to make a life for myself." He took a puff from his cigar. "You know, I'll probably end up like old Rusty, cursing the horses and eating dust all day, but I've dreamed of driving the coaches since I was no bigger than Fuller. Pa insisted I finish school, and he was right, but I'm free now, and I look forward to the new route in the West." He put his cigar out by grinding it into the dirt.

"I wish you well, and I'd like to hear from you occasionally. Write to me when you can." Joe reached and shook his hand, then they separated to join the other people around the station.

The next morning, Hannah and Ruth had breakfast on the

73

table as the guests awoke for their trip to Denver. Willingham shook Joe's hand and thanked him for an enjoyable stay. He glanced toward Standing Tree, but didn't show any emotion on his face; neither did he flinch when Hannah gave him a bright smile and wished him well. The ladies collected their skirts and entered the coach. There was room inside for three of the other men, and one rode on top, hanging on to the rail. Matthew Baldwin, with a last wave of the hand, followed the ladies inside, and Joe closed the door. Ivan climbed into the box; Hank took his seat with his shotgun on his lap, and the wheels began to roll. Joe felt a huge lump in his throat as they passed under the cottonwoods and willows. Hannah came to stand beside him, a tear in her eyes, and Joe gave her a hug.

It wasn't until later that Joe had a chance to examine a box that had arrived on the coach for him from Denver. It had inside the new suit purchased for Peter and the smaller suit for Fuller. He smiled. "So Ambrosine was honest after all." He found a folded piece of paper inside the brown paper in which the smaller suit was wrapped. "Mr. Hadley, sir. I am Israel Bodkin, from Poland, in the United States for ten years now. Ambrosine says you live in an isolated area and have no tailor nearby. I am thankful for your business and am sending a catalog for your perusal." It was signed with a flourish, and Joe laughed out loud.

"Hannah, come here." She looked up from the water color painting she was finishing at the table. She quickly washed her brush in the bowl of water and dried it.

"What is it, honey? You seem excited." She looked at the brown wrapping paper he had strewn across the floor.

"It's Papa's suit, and the one for Fuller."

She frowned.

"You remember the man who was here a few months back. He had a catalog with pictures of men's suits and ties." He handed her the catalog that Bodkin had enclosed in the package. She gave it back to him without looking inside.

"Well, botheration. Does he think you and Papa go to the opera every week? What do you need a suit for?" But, Joe wasn't really listening. He was thumbing through the catalog and found some pages with men's long wool coats.

"Look, Hannah. We could use new overcoats. I like this style. What do you think?" And, before she could answer, he was turning to the order form at the back of the catalog. She gave an exasperated sigh and went back to her painting.

Six

"Papa, I need your advice. I've seen you with the Indian. I think you've made a special bond, and I've seen how he responds to you. Have you any suggestions for bringing him back to the security he once felt among us?"

"Hm." Peter pulled his cigar from his mouth and pursed his lips, thinking, before he blew out a long stream of smoke. Then he nodded, and pointing at Joe with his cigar, he spoke a solution that Joe was surprised he hadn't thought of.

"Stimulation is what the man needs. The leg injury might seem to some to be the cause of his melancholy mood, and I know you hoped for a swift recovery, but well, sometimes wounds don't heal as well as we want. You can't expect a man used to action to lay around all day and still be the man he wants to be. How about a hunting party?" His eyes twinkled, and Joe suspected his father would like to go on one as well.

"Are you sure, Papa? I might have to take you along to see that I don't overtax Standing Tree's recently healed leg." It was a tease, and he chuckled.

"You might have to insist, but I think I'll give in, if you

press me hard enough." Peter laughed and clasped his hand on his son's shoulder.

It took some time to set up the hunt, but Joe and Peter, with Standing Tree as guide and tracker, started off one morning in October with a pack on one of the donkeys to look for signs of deer or antelope. They moved deep into the forest until they came to a clearing with a shallow stream, where they set up a shelter of dried limbs and boughs. They covered it with leaves and sod dug from the bank of the creek. They waited, half hidden by the enclosure. There was little talk between the men, and that was undertaken in whispers. The wind was calm, but the night air chilled and damp. The sound of the rushing waters of the creek seemed soothing after their long ride from the station.

Just before sunset, Standing Tree sat forward, as though he heard something the other two men didn't hear. He raised his hand for quiet. The men sat as stones. At the edge of the clearing, a buck appeared. He raised his head and sniffed the wind, as though testing for danger. Peter's eyes glowed with excitement, while the Indian remained still and watchful. Joe gazed in wonder at the majesty and pride of the animal.

Standing Tree signed to Joe and pointed to the shadows near the tree line. Three does came marching in formation, one at a time, and stopped to nibble on the verdant grass. One fine doe was followed by a fawn. They moved sedately from one place to another, as though they were taking a leisurely stroll through the late afternoon air. The buck dropped his head to munch on the grass and then moved to the stream for water. One of the does wandered to the edge of the trees and browsed alone.

It was a perfect opportunity, but Joe hesitated to disturb the family scene. On the other hand, he knew that the station needed fresh meat, and that Standing Tree was deserving of the glory of the hunt. It was the very reason he and his father had brought him along.

Joe moved cautiously forward and made hand gestures that the Indian should make the kill. Standing Tree gestured that he understood and drew an arrow from his quiver and stretched it to its full length in the circle of the bow. With a whishing sound the arrow sailed through the air, and the doe fell to her knees. Another arrow pierced her heart, and she lay still. The buck made an angry, roaring sound and instantly the other does and the fawn took off into the woods. The buck stayed a moment longer, as if puzzled why the female didn't arise and run away. He then bounded away and was soon lost in the darkness.

Without a word, Standing Tree rushed to the doe and used his knife with dexterity and haste, cutting the animal's throat, and starting to peel away the skin. Peter watched, remarking to Joe, "I hardly knew what I'd feel, but I'm stunned by the rise of emotions that are filling my chest. One moment there is a magnificent animal, proud and sovereign in his kingdom; and in an instant his peace is destroyed by man."

"I agree with you, Papa, but man must eat and the skin won't be wasted. You see how Standing Tree is removing it in one piece. The deer's life will be of use even after the meat is gone."

Joe remembered they had hunted often in Indiana for meat, and his father hadn't questioned the need for food then. He left his father with his thoughts, and moved forward to help the Indian skin the animal and cut the meat. They placed it in the old canvas bags they had brought with them, and tied the bags securely to the donkey's pack, leaving a good-sized part for their supper.

Peter roused himself into action and built a fire with twigs and leaves. The men finished the dressing of the meat and ate a hearty supper of roasted venison and some of Hannah's cold biscuits. They drank cool water from the stream, rolled into their blankets and slept.

It took some minutes for the men to pack up all they had brought with them, adding it to the donkey's pack, but soon they were on their way home. It seemed Standing Tree's good humor was restored, just as Joe hoped, and they had more good food to eat in addition.

When the men returned from the hunt, Joe and Peter, with the help of Standing Tree, scraped the deer skin until it was soft and pliable. He cut off a square and gave the rest to the Indian, telling him in the half sign language communication that seemed to work for them, "For you, Standing Tree. Make moccasins. Last long time. I wish vest shirt for boy with rest. Fine with you?" He hoped the Indian understood. He fancied his son standing in a law court someday with the buckskin vest under his suit coat.

"Is fine with Standing Tree. Boy need. Hide will last many years." He grinned broadly, taking the larger portion, then grasping the part Joe had kept back and shaking it. He pushed it back to Joe with a laugh.

*****

In the last days of October, the coach from the south with Jim Owens driving and Fizzure Rodriguez serving as shotgun messenger arrived with a "Hallo, the house!" and five passengers, a father, mother and three children, the oldest being a boy of about eight years. As soon as the coach stopped, and the doors were opened, the child bolted like a spring-born fawn, and was almost immediately off to the corrals and running through the barn with abandon.

"Dereck," his mother Carolina Milnor called. "I told you in the coach that you must do better." She looked at her husband but only received a minor rebuke for the boy from the harried-looking man.

"Boy! Better listen to your ma!" His attention immediately went to the younger two, and they seemed to be at loose ends, also.

"Dereck," his mother said again, chasing after him. "I will not warn you again. You make your way to the house before I swat your behind." The Milnor family made their way with some difficulty and disruption towards the house, the father, Piney, arriving first with the two youngest, and the mother with her son by the ear.

Joe hardly had an opinion on the matter, because the family hadn't let him get in a word of greeting. He followed them, hoping Hannah had better luck getting their attention.

Sometime later, Slim showed up at the house, carrying the boy, telling Joe he was attending to the foal when he heard a thump and a loud scream from the lad. Running to the sound he saw the boy had fallen from the ladder leading to the loft. He saw the strange angle of his arm and knew that it was broken.

Joe instructed Slim to lay him on the table, after telling Ruth to remove the contents. Hannah was feeding Fuller his dinner before putting him to bed for the night, and she bustled the boy off beside the fireplace, so as not to disturb the men. By the light of the lantern, Slim used a flat board and clean bandages to set the arm while the mother hovered over the boy, weeping and wringing her hands. The two girls stared wide-eyed at their brother. The father came in from the bunkhouse where he had been playing poker with Ivan and Hank, saw his wife upset, and began to threaten Slim, Joe and everyone else that lived at the station.

Joe set the man straight, telling him he had been in the far field with Peter gathering the last of the corn crop, only arriving at the house when Slim had brought the boy in.

"I knew nothing of your son's whereabouts, sir, and was waiting until supper was served. The station is safe for supervised children, but it is a working stagecoach station. Your watchfulness over your son is your best bet to prevent injury."

The man still spat and growled, but Joe knew where he'd been.

"Sir, calm down. Your boy will be fine; just a slight fracture of the arm. He'll be uncomfortable for a while but soon healed. There's no reason why you can't continue on your way on the stage tomorrow." Slim tried to defuse the situation, but the man continued to threaten.

With the courage and daring of a real pioneer, Hannah gave her son into the arms of her mother-in-law, withdrew the small pistol she carried in her apron pocket and pointed it at the man.

"Sir, you will stop this nonsense at once. You are scaring your children and my son. I will not have such behavior in my home. Since you can't leave the station tonight, you can return to the bunkhouse until you apologize to the animal handler, who possibly saved your boy's life with his skill and fast action." The merchant opened his mouth to object, but his wife, with her hysteria under control, spoke first.

"Piney, Mrs. Hadley is right. All this bluster and threats don't accomplish anything but frighten the children. If Dr. Grimshaw is finished, take Dereck into our bedroom where I can sit with him while he sleeps." As though a flash of lightning had come from above, the man's manner changed. He apologized to Slim and the women, lifted his son and carried him from the room. He sat at the dinner table, subdued, and ate with vigor. Hannah carried a tray to the bedroom for the wife.

A couple of hours later, the northbound stage arrived with two more passengers. The two merchants talked quietly while Peter read from a book beside the fireplace. Standing Tree sat in his place on the floor. The children sat at the table coloring on Hannah's lined tablet paper, while she showed them how to make circles, squares and loops with the different colored pencils.

Joe didn't speak of the incident until he and Hannah were alone in their room. The affair was finished, so he said nothing the next morning when the family prepared to board the stage for the next station which was Buckboard. The boy was quiet and his arm held tight against his chest in a sling. Slim said not a word as he held the reins while Joe did his usual check of animals and coach. He made sure the axles were greased, put the luggage into the rear boot, and wished Ivan and Hank God's speed. He watched with an odd look on his face, as the coach disappeared down the forest road. He turned and went back to gathering the corn crop to be put in the crib for winter.

Seven

The last freight caravan of the season came through in mid-November and brought the Denver and St. Louis newspapers. It was mostly old news, but welcome to the isolated residents of the station: the first shipment of cattle to the East occurred on the Kansas Pacific Railroad, as herds continued to arrive from Texas on the Chisholm Trail; President Johnson proclaimed unconditional pardon and amnesty without reservations for most of those accused of treason against the Union during the Civil War; the election of General Ulysses S. Grant as the new president, taking the place of President Andrew Johnson who was acquitted by the Senate in his impeachment trial; the purchase of Alaska; the ratification of the Fourteenth Amendment, giving the rights of citizenship to the former slaves; and in the local news, a house burned down, killing a child within its walls.

The people of Sweetwater debated and discussed the events for days until everyone was tired of the subjects, but no general consensus on how to effectively change any matters that were not directly related to the station was reached, and with a general feeling of relief, they one by one ceased to mention them.

The family welcomed the supplies to carry them over the winter months, bacon, sausage, fruit and tobacco, tooth powder and boot polish. Of special importance to the ladies were fresh linens for the beds, soap and yarn for making scarves and caps. Included were several pairs of trousers in various sizes for the men, shoes for the ladies, and books. The women pounced on the copy of Louisa Mae Alcott's *Little Women* and the men over the latest Horatio Alger release.

A week later, a blizzard of major proportion blew in from the north and the station was covered in snow for four days, before the sun came out and melted it away. A rope was strung between the buildings for the men to follow, so they could cross from one to the other without getting lost in the white powder. Peter took supplies to the large room so the men wouldn't have to cross to the house for all their meals. Surprisingly, Hank turned into a fair cook and his coffee was praised by the other men.

Joe was torn between caring for the animals and worry over his wife. On the Thursday of that terrible week, while sitting at the table for the evening meal, Hannah cried out, "Joe. Something's wrong."

"Let me help you to bed." He was at her side immediately, but when she stood, she bent over, and a puddle appeared at her feet.

"No, it isn't time. The baby cannot come now." She gasped and held onto Joe's arm. "Mama, I need your help."

Ruth put aside the skillet she was using and rushed to Hannah's side. "This baby is coming now." She told Joe to boil some water and bring the shears and a blanket.

Joe felt helpless to do as she said. "I can go for Slim." He considered the problem with that. The snow was packed around the buildings, and he didn't know if the rope was still attached. Anyway, he needed to be with Hannah to help her through this time. Even Standing Tree was in the bunkhouse and unable to offer his version of medicinal advice. He didn't expect his father would stand the exposure without a detrimental effect on his health.

"There's no time. You have to help me now." Hannah dropped to her knees, pushing the table aside some, and rolling to her side. "Joe, get cloths." She gasped with pain. Peter rushed up with a couple of blankets from a guest bedroom, and retreated to the fireplace area.

She was delivered of a tiny girl who didn't survive the night.

Joe and Peter built a small coffin and waited until the snow melted to bury her beside Jeremiah Fuller under a carpet of fallen pine needles and cones. The surface of the ground was frozen and covered with melting snow, but they managed to dig deeply enough that wild animals wouldn't have a chance at the body. They piled rocks on top so they would find the mound when they could have a memorial service and chisel a marker. They gave her the name Anne after Hannah's mother.

Hannah sat quietly in the rocking chair for another week, her health restored, but not her spirit. Her sorrow was so deeply felt that Joe couldn't comfort her. She withdrew from his loving arms. Finally, with the understanding that only a mother can give, Ruth stepped in.

"Hannah, you are right to grieve. You've suffered a great loss." Ruth patted her arm, and after a moment, she rubbed her cold hand to warm it. "What's done is done, and the child won't come back. You must finish your public grieving and take care of your son, who needs you. You can grieve in private, and I expect you'll do so, but this isn't the time. I'm sorry, my dear, but this is the way it must be."

Tears flowed from Hannah's eyes as Ruth spoke. Joe watched his mother work her magic, as Hannah stood and walked to Fuller, picking him up and sitting with him on the couch. She began to hum a familiar tune, but she didn't speak. Later that evening, she donned her apron and stepped to the stove, and she began to prepare dough for the next morning's biscuits.

"I love you, wife." Joe stepped behind her and moved a strand of hair from her neck to kiss it. He wanted to do more, but didn't dare risk her fragile condition.

"I so wanted her, that's all. Please let me get this dough prepared. I'll be alright. Really I will." She didn't turn to him, but Joe could tell things would be better.

Wolves howled in the night, and the wind whistled through the tall pines and cottonwoods. Standing Tree was given a room in the bunkhouse, but he slept on the floor near the fireplace, covered with blankets. He had recovered from his illness, but was slow in his movements. He developed a deep cough, but Slim said it wasn't serious.

By Sunday morning of the last week of November, a weak sun appeared and slowly brightened as the day wore on. By afternoon the snow began to melt in earnest, and Hannah fully helped Ruth with the evening meal, from the beginning to the end, and was even able to smile as she placed the prepared items on the table. The men rejoiced as they were able to cross without stumbling in the slush of snow and mud. Normality was restored and the wolves stopped howling as suddenly as they had appeared, with no loss to the livestock.

December dawned bright and cheerful. The days grew warm and the snow melted away. A stage made it through from the south with Jim Owens driving and Fizzure Rodriguez as guard, identifying itself with, "Hallo, the house!" Inside were three men on their way to Denver.

"How was your trip?" Joe quizzed them over a hot meal.

"Frightening," one who had been introduced as Tom Gibbons commented. "The mud splatters up, and in places snow still fills the low places. My friend here, Gerand Womble, is worried that it may be worse toward Denver. He wants to continue on. I feel he may be correct, although with your wife's good cooking, to be stranded here doesn't seem so dreadful as it did while riding in the coach." He laughed.

The third man was Gifford Isinghouse, and he slapped his fist on the table. "Weather! If we weren't in dire need of our Denver accommodations, I would return to Atlanta in a fortnight and remain where it only snows when we wish it to snow."

Gibbons laughed in a jolly manner, and he clapped Isinghouse on the shoulder. "I am sure you would, but you're a businessman, just as Gerand and myself, and you would make no money in Atlanta. So, we are headed to Denver."

Joe found the men quite pleasant, and he wouldn't have minded them staying overnight, but he understood their urgency. They didn't want to chance being on the road in case of more bad weather. Ivan and Hank headed out with them onboard, and returned early the next day with news that the roof of the barn at Rockland Station had collapsed during the snow storm, and one of the horses had been crushed. Moore and Jane were well and the rest of the station stock had come through the storm without harm.

January and February were cold and wet, but no more blizzard conditions arrived. One day the rain turned to ice during the night and a couple of the chickens froze in their coop. Slim was kept busy with a horse that tore his leg on a fence log. Several tree limbs fell onto the ground from the weight of the ice on their branches. As soon as he could, Joe cut them into firewood. The men played poker and other table games in the large room of the bunkhouse and read the newspapers and magazines over again, with the same news. A lively game with dice kept them entertained one evening until after midnight, with friendly ribbing the next morning for the faint of heart.

Hannah and Ruth fingered the pictures of the ladies' fashions in the magazines. Ruth remarked, "I remember Rebecca and Emily. How grand they looked, even from their ride in the coach."

"And the other ladies," Hannah added. "There are so many we've known who have traveled along the route to Denver or St. Louis. They remind me of life in the city, when I lived with my uncle. I wasn't happy then, but there was no end to all the goings on. It was very lively." She giggled like a girl when she said that, looking at Joe.

"I heard you, wife." He wagged his finger at her, but he did it with a smile. "You were glad to be rescued, and you were glad it was me."

"I'm glad it was you." Ruth placed her hand on Hannah's arm, whispering rather over loudly to her.

"I'll be glad of a bite to eat, especially if it's hot." Joe teased.

The women sighed and rose to cook the meal for their menfolk. Over the weeks, Hannah taught Fuller a few simple words and he repeated them like a parrot. Ivan carved a wagon with spinning wheels out of a fallen spruce limb, and tied a cord to the front. The boy raced through the Public Room and became frustrated when the wagon tipped over and stopped him from his journey. Standing Tree took some bits of deer skin and made moccasins for Joe and Peter, and Hannah sewed beads on them from the box that Joe had brought from Denver. He collected a few limbs and made new arrows for his bow. He lamented the fact that it was too cold for fishing or hunting.

At last, when the residents had read all the books, newspapers and magazines until the pages were ragged and torn, the sun shone in earnest.

"Ah," Hannah remarked, standing next to Joe with the sun in her face. "I've needed this."

"You've had a hard season." He put an arm across her shoulders and squeezed her. He was pleased to feel her head resting against him.

"I would like to go up to see where Anne is buried when the ground dries. I would like to plant some flowers to make it pretty."

That was when Joe knew Hannah was truly past the worst of the tragedy that had overtaken her with the loss of the child.

Soon the edges of the spring thawed, and the creek flowed freely through the fields of early spring blooming flowers. One afternoon, Joe called to his father, "Papa, I do believe the chickens need some space to wander and get some exercise." Together, with much laughing at the flying feathers and squawking birds, they released the chickens to peck in the ground for their food. Fuller saw the activities, and now well-adjusted to his growing legs, he chased the birds back and forth across the yard. Joe gathered him in his arms and swung him around to the boy's great delight. He carried him into the house.

The horses seemed to step more lively around the corrals, and the grass grew green and tall around the walls of the barn, outhouse and sheds. Joe cut it down and fed it to the mules and goats. Peter got out the sharpening stone and honed the plow. His fingers itched, he said, to dig in the dirt once again.

Fuller was now as tall as Joe's waist and would pull himself onto the table to grab at the biscuits or food if Hannah didn't see him in time.

"No," she called to him one time, pushing his hand away. His face balled up, and his eyes grew red with tears. Ruth had to turn away, so she wouldn't get involved. He whined and cried, and eventually Hannah swept him up and cuddled him in her arms. The color had returned to her cheeks and she spent more time with the boy, while Ruth did the household work she was able to do with her painful hands. She no longer did any needle work. Slim and Peter did the milking of the nanny goat and collecting the eggs.

On the third of March, Ivan and Hank brought visitors on the westbound headed for Mozier Station. On board the stage were two sisters and their husbands, and a boy of about fourteen years with a curiosity as large as the sky. They were introduced as Franklin and Gilda Radkin, Simmie and Pet Macanese, and Chaddie Macanese. The boy poked and pried in all the buildings and doors until Joe was forced to set some boundaries for him. His father laughed, calling out, "Are you finding any new things, Chaddie?"

Joe gave him a piercing gaze and the man sobered, calling his boy back, and telling him, "The man is right, boy. There are things here that are not ours, and we must abide by his rules."

Still, Chaddie pouted, and he kicked at the ground. When he got some dirt on his father, the man yanked his arm, and sent him to sit against the wall.

Once in the house, Franklin Radkin called out with audacity, "Mrs. Hadley, is that a birthmark on your face?"

His wife tittered, but she doused it quickly and slapped her husband on the arm, telling him, "You are so rude, Mr. Radkin. I told you not to say anything." She looked interested in Hannah's response, though.

"I was burned in the house fire which took the lives of my parents." Hannah didn't say more, just turned to her stove and continued to work.

The group seemed more subdued after her response, and Pet Macanese gave her a hug. "I'm sorry, my dear. It's been a long trip, and we've been cooped up with each other far too long. We've forgotten how to be polite to others. Will you accept my apologies?"

"Thank you." Hannah nodded her head, and the woman moved away.

Hannah served a ham with her special tart sauce, potatoes, turnips with their greens and hot corn on the cob. Apple pie was served and small chunks of Ruth's goat cheese with the last of the walnuts and pecans from the November freight wagons from Denver.

The conversation flowed easily among guests and hosts, and the evening went well after that. Still, it was with some relief when the guests climbed aboard the coach the next day, chatting among themselves about the excellent breakfast Hannah had served.

As the horn blew, signaling the departing stage, Hannah waved good-bye, no longer troubled by the rudeness of the day before.

Eight

Hannah awoke early as was her custom, dressed and went to the stove to begin her day. When the flame was reduced to a slow, steady glow, she filled the coffee pot with grounds and water, and set it on the burner. She smiled when Joe came into the room, a sleepy Fuller in his arms. She took the child and placed him in his tall chair, while Joe went to light the fireplace. There was a nip in the air, and from the window he could see a fog on the spring and creek. He went out to the mountain of firewood and brought in an armload, then went for more. When the box was full to overflowing, he went out to begin the process of sending the guests on their way to the next station. He left the dog roaming in the yard, following some mysterious scent.

He went into the bunkhouse first and knocked on Ivan's door. "Ivan, time to get up. Coffee's hot." He passed on to Hank's room but was thwarted by the opening of the door.

"I know, Boss, coffee's hot." It was a joke between the men; a signal of sorts that Hannah was cooking breakfast. He grinned at Joe and finished buttoning his shirt. He lifted his coat and hat from the pegs on the wall near the door, and waited as Joe went to the fourth door in the hallway. They saw Ivan leave the building for the corral.

He knocked, "Walton, breakfast in an hour. Take your time, though, the stage won't be here until late afternoon." He joined Hank, not waiting for the visitor to respond. He either came to eat or went hungry. The decision was left to the passengers. Since he didn't expect Jim Owens and Rodriguez until near sunset, the man would find his own entertainment during the day. The single men were offered books, outdated magazines, playing cards and board games in the large bunkhouse room or a stroll of the grounds and talking with the residents.

The other guests were more important, since they would be taking Rusty's coach that arrived shortly after the noon meal to the Mozier station. Only in the last few months had guests come from the west in large numbers. Usually, they were traveling to Denver or points south. It was what he and Ned Baldwin had discussed many times in person and by letter when the Eastern Division Agent was in charge of the stations when Joe first started working for the stage line. As he reached Slim's room, he opened the door, and without a word, joined Hank and Joe as they exited the bunkhouse. Hank headed for the house and his meal, while Slim and Joe went to the corrals. They stopped first at the barn.

Inside the surgery section, Slim checked an injured horse and found him not breathing. A loud, long stream of curses flowed freely from his mouth. He was one of the yearlings captured in last year's mustang hunt that he had kept for breeding.

"I swear, Joe, he was fine when I left him early in the morning. I should have stayed with him. Damn. There must have been an infection that I didn't catch. I'm sorry."

"Don't fret. It wasn't your fault. These things happen. We'll select the mules for Rusty's coach and the horses for the northbound, and after breakfast we'll take him into the forest." The men left the barn and went to the corrals to select the animals for the coaches. They left them in the holding pens while they went to eat. Joe saw his father leave the house for his first smoke of the day.

"Papa, we lost the mustang yearling that Slim was tending. We'll need your help with hauling him to the forest for burial. Are the guests up and stirring?" Joe looked closely at his father. He appeared haggard, as though he hadn't slept well.

"That's too bad, son." Peter looked at Slim. "Come with me to milk the nanny. I want to talk to you about something." Joe looked at him, but he didn't indicate that he was included in the conversation, so he turned and went to the house.

Hannah and Ruth were busy at the stove, and one of the guests was sitting at the table. Mamie Luz, Joe thought, and he sat down to listen to their conversation. Hannah brought a cup and the coffee pot and poured some of the hot, fragrant brew into the cup. The woman was talking about the women's suffrage movement. Joe kept his eyes down. He chuckled to himself. He grasped that the woman was wrapping up her spiel to gain the approval of the station women.

He finished his cup of coffee and took Fuller from his chair, pleased to leave them to their discussion. He noticed that Hannah smiled at him. He smiled back and helped his son with his outer garments. He went first to the outhouse and then set the toddler on his feet to walk uncertainly through the grass. He stood and watched as Fuller and Jack rambled around in the still damp yard. Standing Tree was sitting under the tree, smoking his pipe.

"'Morning, my friend." He made the sign of the early sun rising and took a deep breath, patted his chest and pointed to the distant mountains. "A good day for hunting. Young brown horse die in barn. Take to the forest, later."

The Indian grunted and walked toward the house. Joe noticed he was no longer limping. That was good. He'd worried about the old man. He watched Fuller and Jack a few more minutes and called for his son to come to him. He lifted him on his shoulders, and the lad squealed in pleasure. The dog wagged his tail and barked. They caught up to Peter coming from the goat shed, a bucket of milk in one hand. Joe lifted an eyebrow in question, but his father didn't speak. He called to the dog, who followed him meekly into the Public Room.

The table was full of people eating and talking. Joe removed the lad's outer garments and took him to the bedroom to pull off his shoes and put tiny moccasins on his feet. He dried his feet and made sure his trousers legs weren't damp. They were; so he changed the boy's trousers and combed his hair. He took pleasure in his son and talked to him in a calm voice, speaking his thoughts out loud as though the boy was much older. He explained about the guests and the need to be quiet and not distract his mama from her work. He took a picture book from the shelf with him to the Public Room for the boy's entertainment after his meal.

Joe was now acquainted with the guests, having spoken to them after dinner the previous night. He fed his son some porridge and smashed eggs, while they continued their conversation. He noticed Walton kept glancing at Standing Tree, eating in his regular place. Ivan and Hank very seldom took part in the table talk among the guests, but since his conversation with Slim, Joe noticed that he was following the talk of the railroad closely. The talk moved on to the creation of a baseball team. Joe was fascinated by the subject as Bart Luz and Archie Gillian, the passengers, took turns explaining the movements and scoring of the game. Slim asked if it was similar to the games played in England with a bat, and told the difference. The conversation continued for some time, the men moving from the dining table to the outdoors area, with a demonstration of the game.

Joe motioned for Slim and Peter to follow him. Standing Tree moved outside and followed to the barn, where he squatted near the entrance. He knew the men would rather hear about the game of baseball, but they had work to do. With a sigh, Peter grabbed a long rope off a shelf in the supply room, and the men dragged the carcass of the horse out the back door of the barn, hoping to keep their actions hidden from the guests, and into the forest where Joe dug a pit for it. Slim helped him fill in the pit, while Peter took the rope back to the barn and hitched two mules to the plow.

The men were still running around in the yard, and Joe went to the holding pen to examine the horses and mules they had selected for the coaches. When he finished to his satisfaction, he lit a fire in the pit, for he knew the women would want to wash the bed linens. He noticed that Slim had selected three horses for shoeing and was setting up the forge near the barn. One of the men left their game and followed him. Joe grinned. The other two seemed to tire of the game, and wandered to the spring. Standing Tree took off into the forest with his bow and arrow pouch on his back, his food bag on his hip.

He lifted the huge iron tub onto the fire and hauled water from the spring to fill it. Putting the bucket on the ground nearby, he tended the fire until Hannah came out with a basket of dirty clothing and bed linens. She had an exasperated look on her face and laughed.

"Joe, I have to warn you, your mother and I will want to vote when the Congress passes the bill for women's suffrage. Mrs. Luz has convinced me that our lot is desperate. We can't let the men keep control over us. We have to stand up for our rights as citizens, you know. Poor Mama is being tormented by that woman. I'll be glad when Rusty gets here."

"Are you serious? Should I go rescue Mama? Lordy, I don't know what I can do. Do you think the women should have the vote?" He looked at his wife with a speculative gaze, and before she could answer went to the side wall where he lifted the wash tubs down and brought them one at a time to the pit area.

"I guess it would be a good thing for the women, but I dread the men's reaction. Where would we vote, Joe? Would we have to go into Denver? That's a long trip. You and Slim and Papa don't vote."

Joe looked at Slim, now pounding on a horseshoe nail. The other two men had wandered over to watch him.

"I never even thought of it before. I suppose Papa voted in Indiana, but I wasn't old enough when I went into the Army. I suppose we'd have to go to Denver, but would it be worth the trip and the length of time away from the station? Maybe Jameson was right, maybe we should move to Denver. You and Mama could go the opera and the museums."

"Now, you stop this talk, my husband. We're not moving to Denver. You've just bought this place and here we'll stay, even if the stage line shuts us down. We have the animals, the land and the forest if we need to sell off some timber—"

Joe threw his head back and laughed until his sides ached.

Hannah stared at him and began to laugh herself. The washing was temporarily forgotten. He eventually sobered and gave her a hug.

"I love you, my beautiful wife," he said in her ear and stepped back to admire the blush on her cheeks.

"I love you, too." She gazed into his eyes a moment longer, and turned to the house. "You wait right there, Mr. Hadley. I have another basket of clothes to wash." She flounced to the front door and entered the house. His eyes followed her until she disappeared inside, and he turned to dip the bucket into the hot water and filled the first tub.

When Hannah returned, carrying a basket piled high with soiled clothing in her arms, she was accompanied by Ruth holding Fuller in her arms. Joe looked closely at his mother and saw what Hannah had indicated. Ruth was trying her best to hold her temper.

"Go ahead, Mama, spill it out before you explode. If the women are troubling you, I'll tell them to stay in their rooms."

"No. It's alright. As long as we stay busy, I think they'll leave us be. The one called Mamie said she had some letters to write. I gave her paper and pens. Joe, get me a chair and I'll watch Fuller while you and Hannah work."

Joe went to do his mother's bidding. He went in the front door and saw the lady called Mamie busy at the table writing her letters; the other one wasn't there, and he assumed she'd gone to her room. He picked up one of the chairs and took it to his mother.

Hannah was stirring the first batch of clothing in the tub of sudsy water when he returned. Ruth put Fuller on the ground and sat in the chair.

"Now, son, bring me that bucket of potatoes and I'll keep

myself busy here."

Once more, Joe went to the kitchen, found the bucket of potatoes and an empty one for the rinds, and picked up a small knife. He stopped in his tracks when Mamie Luz spoke.

"Mr. Hadley, what do you think of women's suffrage?"

"I'm all for it, ma'am, but have you considered that most people live in rural areas like this one? Where would Hannah and my mother vote? It'd be long hours on the stage into Denver; or we might be in the district south of here instead, near Trinidad. The stage only runs once a week. What if it doesn't run on Election Day? Would we have the expense of a hotel room and meals while waiting for the polls to open? It might take us three or four days in order to get to vote. I think it's a fine idea for you city people, but when you discuss it with your leaders, consider the other women of the country as well, please." He turned and left the woman staring at him.

Feeling slightly guilty, Joe hovered over the area the rest of the morning, helping with the clothes hanging. The dog wandered from tree to tree and over to the goat shed and back. He noticed Hannah needed more space, so he went to a pile of limbs waiting to be cut into firewood and strung another line from the post to the tree. There was a small area at one end, large enough for socks or small items. Soon, the lines were full of bed sheets and clothing flapping and drying in the warm sunshine.

Standing Tree was gone all day, and Joe began to worry, but he knew there was nothing to be done. He examined the harness minutely for damage and helped Slim with horse shoeing when asked. He watched the men wander the area, and when the women finished their task and went to fix the noon meal, they moved to the barn. Joe talked to them of the mustang hunts and the breeding of the animals. He told them something of the first days, when Jackson's crew was building the road through the forest and the building of the brick barn. He laughed at that. He, Buck Jones and Jeremiah Fuller had laid them all, one at a time, while Rosie Jones had made hundreds of bricks near the creek banks.

The dinner was mostly beans, cornbread, onions and left over roast from the night before, but it was filling, and the people had barely finished when the sound of a blaring trumpet playing an army tune was heard. It was Rusty and Grover. The dog set to barking and wagging his tail, and Joe quietly told his guests to collect their possessions. With such a large group of people, the station wouldn't have room for all to stay the night. They must catch the stage when it left.

Joe and Slim went to the coach, leaving Hannah and Ruth to set clean plates and glasses on the table. Before he was there, the door opened and a heavy-set man stepped down. He was followed by a woman in silks and large brimmed hat with a white feather. An older woman followed her and last, a tall, thin man in a dark suit.

"Welcome to Sweetwater. Please, join us in the house for dinner. My wife and mother are waiting to welcome you." He turned to Rusty, and helped him down from the box.

"Let me go. I ain't so stove up that I can't get down on my own. How ya been? How's that young'un of yores?" Rusty watched as the guests went into the house and turned to Slim. "Better see to that right wheelhorse, Slim. He's limping. Damn sand was blowing like a fury; dirt devils everywhere, I could just make out the road." He opened his eyes wide when the two men, Luz and Gillian, emerged from the house. It was still unusual for people to ride from west to east.

100

"You have riders for the east, Rusty, at least five of them; I think the other is headed south; maybe ride with Owens, or Ward if they come. We don't have space for everyone to stay the night." He looked at Grover, standing with the shotgun in the crook of his left arm. "If you're too tired to drive further, Grover can do it, I suppose."

Rusty let out a string of oaths loud enough to call the birds out of the nearby trees. They flew away with a flutter of wings. He stopped when Luz and Gillian were close enough to hear them.

"You headed to Mozier Station? Got your luggage handy? We'll leave in about an hour, soon's we get a fresh team and eat our dinner." He held out his hand. "Name's Rusty Backgammon, this here's Grover; he'll be driving the stage." And, with a wink at Joe, he headed to the outhouse. Grover shook hands and walked into the house for his meal, his eyes gazing into Joe's as he passed. He grinned.

While this was going on, Slim had unhitched the team and led them to the water trough. Joe went to help him. The two men followed. Joe explained to the men why mules were used on the route between Sweetwater and Mozier, that it was because of the deep sandy bogs. As he was speaking, he checked the mules for cuts, bruises or abrasions from the harness. From the mules, he went to the coach, giving it a thorough going-over and greased the axles. The men asked questions, and he answered them truthfully. Slim then led the new team to the stage and hitched them, and the process started again. Working as an experienced team, even with the men watching, the work was finished by the time Rusty came from the house, his ever present cigar in his mouth. He took a deep puff and took Joe's arm to draw him aside.

"Joe, we've heard rumors the railroad is built through to Denver. Is that true? Word down the line says we ain't got jobs soon."

"Yes, I'm afraid it's true, my friend. When I was in Denver, I talked to Tisdale about it. He figures by June the Union Pacific from Nebraska will be joined with the Central Pacific from California somewhere in Utah. That won't affect us for a while, but you wait and see, with the Transcontinental Railway finished by next year the stage lines will be cutting back. That's considerable north of us, but if the people of Denver get their line through to connect with the Union Pacific, we're doomed. You might tell Youngblood and his missus, but I'd keep it to myself until we get official word from Tisdale or Baldwin in the East." He stood patiently while Rusty let out another string of curses, enough to curl the hair on a goat's back.

"Damn, Joe. I'm too old to start again somewhere else. What am I to do? Got no family; no real friends 'cept those I work with: you and the Youngbloods and Grover."

"I'm sorry, Rusty, I shouldn't have said so much. Now, you'll be worrying about it. But, there's no need for it. You'll always have a home with us. We'll build you a little cabin, and you can help my father with the garden and the animals." Joe was surprised when Rusty let out another string of curses.

"Dagnabbit, son, I ain't no farmer. But, thanks for the offer. I'll remember it when the time comes. Now, if we're goin' ter make it to Mozier before dark, we'd best get a move on. Roust your passengers out of the house and get their possibles together." He raised his voice. "Grover, get out here, we gotta' go." He turned back to Joe. "Don't fret yourself, my friend, I been taking care of this old man since before you wus even born. I thank you for the information. At least I know what's comin'. It's tha not knowing that drives a man crazy in the night." He started his routine of examining the coach and the mules.

It was Rusty who had taught Joe the importance of caring for the animals and stages at his station. He was grateful and would take care of the old man, if need be.

Grover came from the house, followed by the men with the ladies and their carpetbags. Joe helped put their luggage in the rear boot, shook hands with the men and helped the ladies into the coach and shut the door. Walton remained behind. Grover shook hands with Joe and mounted the box. Rusty climbed aboard onto the high seat with Grover's shotgun in his lap. Joe stepped to the window. He had been with these people for two days and had learned a lot while with them.

"I wish you well on your journey. Thanks for explaining the game of baseball. We'll maybe set up a diamond in the yard and play ourselves." He put his hat back on his head and tipped it to the ladies.

"Giddy-up," shouted Grover, and the team moved forward. Joe stepped back as the sound of Rusty's trumpet carried them across the yard and beyond the grassy fields. He could still hear it as he watched them cross the creek and disappear. He knew with a feeling of sadness that it was Rusty's way of telling him that he would be fine, for he usually played only a few notes. Joe had grown accustomed to the man's choice of music, either joyful or sad or determined. Today, it was an old Irish ballad, and Joe understood the message. He turned to the house to greet his new guests, whom he had left to Hannah and Ruth.

Nine

It was Walton's turn to explain the intricacies of baseball to a new audience. The residents and guests were fascinated, and Joe could tell the man was enjoying the attention without the distraction of the ladies discussing women's suffrage. Since the northbound wasn't due for a couple of hours, and the guests were spending the night, the men, the two new guests named Ferguson and McIlfish, with Walton, Ivan, Hank and Slim played a rousing game of baseball. Since the numbers were even, three against three, Joe didn't play, but watched for a while. They didn't have a ball or bat, so used a sock stuffed with another sock and a tree limb. It was a noisy bunch, and sometime during the afternoon, the word got out that they were actors with a contract to play in the opera house.

Joe was overjoyed with the news, and asked if they would give them a small example of their talent after supper. They hesitated at first, but since they were feeling generous after the game, the older man persuaded his wife to sing for them. They had no instrument, so sang without. First, the lady sang a risqué ditty, then the four sang together and finally, the younger woman sang a sad Italian ballad that left tears in the eyes of everyone, even if they didn't understand the words.

*****

Shortly before sunset, right on schedule, the northbound arrived with Paul Ward driving and Manning as guard. Early the next morning, after eating a large meal, they turned the coach toward the south, taking Walton with them.

Ivan and Hank drove the entertainers to Buckboard and thence to Rockland where they would board the red coach with Rance Potter for Denver.

Standing Tree returned from the forest and said that he'd found the bear tracks, but they stopped near the box canyon. He'd seen signs of Indians crossing the area just south of Buckboard Station. He estimated about a dozen, if Joe interpreted his hand signs correctly. Apache, maybe Comanche, headed south. Joe put out an extra guard each night, and about four days later, Standing Tree awoke Joe. In the early morning mist, they tracked the group to about two miles from the station. They didn't appear hostile; mostly old men, women and children.

"Hungry." Standing Tree pointed to his stomach, his mouth and swallowed. It was similar to the gestures Joe had used when he had first talked to the Indian, found sleeping outside the house wall.

"You come. Not harm Yo Hadley."

The Indian called out in his tongue, and an old man came forward. They used a combination of spoken language and sign to converse, and Standing Tree turned to Joe. "Big man, Apache Woman, Small child, Sammie, Yo Hadley friend, come."

They were a scraggly group dressed in old rags, furs, deerskin, and one had on a Union Army uniform. The Indian walked among them until they came to a woman and boy. She had a baby in a backboard on her back. She was looking down, but Standing Tree pulled her hair and made her raise her head. It was Rosie Jones. He said something to her and she shook her head.

"Rosie, where is Buck? What happened to your husband?" She wouldn't answer, but kept her eyes on the ground.

The old man spoke sharply to her, and she pulled Sammie to her and tried to hide him. Joe could see the fear in her eyes.

"Rosie," he said in a soft voice. "No one will harm you. You remember. I know you do. You remember Standing Tree and Hannah. Tell me what happened to Buck, your husband."

Standing Tree took out his pipe and tobacco and started it going, then offered it to the old man, who looked at it for a moment, then reached out his hand. He signed for Joe to sit down, and he did. Joe had never smoked, but it seemed to be what was required of him, so as the pipe was passed to him he drew in a breath. He blew it out dramatically. The pipe went around the small circle three times, and he pretended to enjoy it, but his stomach was roiling and his head ached.

The old man began to talk; he rambled on; then Standing Tree spoke, and the other man, the one in the Army uniform spoke. Joe didn't know what to say when it came his turn. He started reciting an old poem he had learned in school. It seemed to satisfy the Indians, and they made the rounds again. He recited a different poem. Rosie looked up. The man in the Army uniform said something.

Suddenly, Standing Tree started interpreting for him. "Big Man, Buck, you call; he go to fort with wolf skins; big wagon;

mules; Army catch; put in house with white men. Fight start; man still; dead; Big Man raised high at tree; rope; dead. Rosie run; take Sammie with her. She run, maybe three, four days; find Arapahoe, tell she know Standing Tree; They my people; tell her go to Yo Hadley. They come. You feed; they go away." He pointed toward the south. "Far distance; own land, Apache land."

"Are you saying Buck was captured by the Army and hung from a tree? Are these Apache?"

"Apache, yes. Come to Yo Hadley. Hungry. Go far distance. No come back."

"Rosie, speak to me. Is this true? Buck is dead? These are your people? You need food? Is this Buck's baby? The one on your back? You know you can trust me, Rosie. Remember you made bricks for my barn? Helped Hannah cook? Remember Hannah?"

"Yo Hadley good friend of red man. Buck dead. Baby belong Elk Horns." She pointed to the man in the Army uniform. "He my husband now. We go far away. You help us, Yo Hadley? You help Sammie?"

"Yes, I will help your people. Tell them, Standing Tree. Tell them we will go and bring back food, tobacco, pipes, blankets, clothes. Tell your man, Rosie. I will help."

The old man began to talk, and Joe was puzzled. Was he objecting? Was he testing him?

Rosie spoke. "Yo Hadley, Tomas Big Elk, father of Elk Horns. He say we have nothing give you in return. We poor; no food; no horses. Why you give to us?"

Joe had to think a minute. What could these people give him that was useful to him? Suddenly, he knew. "You tell Elk Horns, I want his coat; the blue coat of the white soldiers." He pointed to the Indian, and signed for him to remove his coat and give it to him. The man gave him an angry growl, but Standing Tree started talking. The old man said something. The man rose, took off his coat and threw it on the ground at Joe's feet and walked away.

Standing Tree said, "We go now; bring back food; clothes; smokes."

Joe followed him back to the station. He went in the house and quickly explained to Peter, then Slim. He showed them the Army coat. He told Hannah what he needed, and they filled a burlap bag with food that he thought the Indians could eat; knowing Standing Tree's preferences, and the loaf of bread that Hannah had baked that day. He put in a separate bag some cobs of corn, a ham and a bag of salt. Rosie would know what to do with it. He took a couple of bags of tobacco and two pipes from his supplies, one for each of the men, and rummaged in his trunk for some old trousers and shirts, an old coat with a patch on one sleeve and several blankets. He waited for Standing Tree and wasn't surprised when the old man showed up with an old bow and a quiver of arrows.

They were weapons for the Indians to use to kill small game.

They carried the bags of food and other supplies to the small clearing, but the people were gone. Standing Tree started tracking and found them a few dozen yards away, hidden in a gulley. Joe surmised they were afraid he would bring back soldiers or other white men to kill them. He pretended he didn't understand. He handed the old man the food and supplies. Standing Tree talked and Rosie came forward.

"Good-bye, Rosie. Take care of your children. I won't forget you." Joe turned to leave. She stopped him. She pulled something from her waist band and held it out to him. It was a small stone. "For Scarred Woman." Joe smiled as he watched the group move toward the south. It was the name Standing Tree called Hannah. Rosie must have picked it up from the Indian. He and Standing Tree went back to the station. He stood near the barn which Buck Jones had helped build and took the stone from his pocket.

Gold! His heart beat like a drum; his hands shook. Surely, it was gold. He'd never seen gold in the raw, but had heard it described. It was small, about the size of a grape, but it was a treasure indeed. With this small stone, the tribe could have eaten for a month. Where had she gotten it? Was this why Buck had been captured by the soldiers? He'd found gold? Joe knew he couldn't keep it; even his friends, Slim, Ivan and Hank wouldn't be able to keep a secret like this for long. He started walking with long strides to the graveyard on the rise above the spring. He knelt in the dirt beside his infant daughter's grave, and dug deep with his hands. He placed the stone there and covered it with soil. It was a secret he intended to keep to his last breath, not even telling Hannah, for whom it was intended.

Ten

March turned to April, and the seeds that Peter planted came up as small green plants. They had hopes of a great harvest. He spent some time in the inner garden between the walls of the house and pulled the weeds and trimmed the bushes. The saplings he had planted were now to the roof of the house and provided shelter for the birds that nested in their branches. Sometimes they were a nuisance and had to be shooed away. But, on most nights when the air was pleasantly warm, Peter and Ruth sat and relaxed in the shade. It was their personal spot, and although Hannah and Joe often joined them, they respected their privacy.

Near the end of April, Rusty came, bringing four passengers, all men. He and Grover didn't stay the night. The evenings were long, and they left to return to Mozier Station. The northbound with Paul Ward driving was expected but didn't arrive, and knowing it didn't travel if there were no passengers, the household went to bed, with Peter taking the first shift as night guard. Joe had early duty the next morning and was sitting near the creek in his favorite spot, where he could see the road south and the eastern flatlands. He thought he saw something move. He stood, poised with his rifle, alert and watchful. It stopped moving and he relaxed.

As though from a far distance, he heard a shout. He gazed toward where he had seen the movement earlier, and heard another shout. He ran to the bunkhouse and pounded on Slim's door.

"Slim, get up and dress. I think I see someone walking toward the station. Hurry, please." He moved to Ivan's door, knocked and repeated his message. By the time he came to Hank's door, it was opened by the man himself.

"What's going on, Joe?" The man stood only in his underpants.

The other doors opened, and he explained to all the men at once. The men started chattering among themselves, but Joe was gone. When he looked to the south again, he was certain it was a man walking. He yelled for Standing Tree to get up and started down to road to meet the man. It was Paul Ward, bloody and bruised; his arm stiff at his side.

"Joe," he managed to get out before he collapsed at the station manager's feet. By this time, Slim and Hank had arrived with Ivan and one of the guests following them. They encircled the injured man.

"Hank, go get the wagon. And, some blankets," Joe thought to add. Hank went on a run back toward the station. Joe took his neckerchief from his neck and wiped the man's face.

"Paul, wake up!" He gently shook him by the shoulders. "Paul." He said louder, "Wake up, man. How can we help you? Tell us what happened." He saw the man's eyes quiver behind his lids and then open. There was a look of terror in his eyes, and he recognized Joe. He blinked and looked around

111

"Hold-up. Some bandits on the road; Manning tried to stop them. He's dead. Two of the passengers dead. They took the woman. I pretended to be dead." He grabbed Joe's arm. "There was nothing I could do, Joe. I didn't have a gun, only the bull whip, and that wouldn't have helped. Go after them, Joe. They have a young woman with them." He closed his eyes, and Joe felt of the vein at the side of his neck to see if he was still alive. It was beating swiftly. He laid him flat and looked toward the station. Slim took over, the closest to a doctor within miles. He took off his shirt and tried to staunch the blood.

One of the strangers started cursing. "Damn bandits. I heard of the James gang from Missouri, but they usually hold up the trains. Who do you think they are, Mr. Hadley?"

"There was an article in the Denver paper last week about the lawless hordes from the war coming west to escape the Federals. Men who rode for Quantrell and worse. Nebraska raiders, too. You think they've gotten this far west?" Another of the strangers had run up in time to join the conversation.

"I don't know. We'll have to send a message to the authorities in Denver. Ivan, go select the horses for your stage. As soon as we get this man to a bed and tend his wounds, the stage'll run to the next station. You guests can be on it. Tell Hannah to hurry along with breakfast and get a bed ready. Try not to frighten the ladies." The coachman walked toward the station. The first stranger who spoke returned with him. They met Hank driving the wagon and said something to him, and continued on. Hank drove steadily on until he came to a stop beside Joe and the other guest.

"What's your name, sir? I don't think I caught it," Joe asked the man who had read the paper, more to distract the man than for information.

"Blandon, sir. Should we move your friend? Looks like he's lost a lot of blood."

"We don't have any choice. We can't leave him here in the dirt. Hank, did you bring some blankets?"

"Yes. I told Hannah to get a big pot of water to boiling and open one of the beds. Didn't know whether you wanted him in the house or the bunkhouse." Hank was breathing fast, and his eyes glowed with excitement. He, Joe and Slim lifted the wounded man and put him in the bed of the wagon. As he was taken from the ground, Joe could see that the stranger was right. There was a large pool of blood left in the soil.

As he was being lifted into the bed of the wagon, Paul groaned and opened his eyes. "The woman. Go find the woman." He fainted again. Joe covered him with the blankets while Slim vaulted to the wagon seat. Blandon climbed on beside Slim, and Hank leaped up beside him. Joe hurled himself into the wagon bed beside Paul, just as Slim started the mules to moving. It wasn't far to the station, and as they moved into the yard, Joe saw the other two strangers standing near the porch. Standing Tree was as still as a pillar under his tree, watching with his black eyes. He started forward as they stopped.

"Go to the bunkhouse, Slim." He yelled, and Slim turned the mules. The wagon clattered toward the large building constructed to house the single workers and guests. He'd suddenly decided they would need the bedrooms in the house for any female passengers while Paul was laid up. He didn't let himself think that his friend might die. He didn't take the time to think of Manning. He jumped from the wagon bed, and helped move Paul into a vacant room.

Slim left the wagon to Ivan or Hank and went to the barn

for his medical bag and the white cloth coat he wore in surgery. "Damn, damn, damn," he muttered to himself. It was beginning to look like he was more a human doctor than a veterinarian. He closed the door of the barn and crossed to the bunkhouse. The room seemed full of people, and he ordered them out.

Joe noticed that Ivan had the big black coach hitched and ready. He was checking the horses' hooves, as he crossed the yard to the house. Hank had told Hannah to get water to boiling in her largest pot, and lots of bandages. Ruth was lifting bacon strips onto a platter. They looked up when Joe came in. The dog was sitting on the floor next to the table. He started barking when Joe came near. He gave him a pat on the head to calm him, and the dog went to lie in his favorite spot by the fireplace, his soft brown eyes watching every movement.

"What's happened? Hank said the northbound stage was robbed and Paul is injured. Where are the others? Manning? The passengers? Joe, tell us something." Hannah's eyes were big with shock and worry, and Joe gave her a hug.

"I'm sorry, dear. I don't know much. Just what Paul said, before he fainted with pain and loss of blood. Slim is with him. He said Manning's dead and two of the male passengers. The bandits took a young woman with them, and I fear the worst. I couldn't bring him in here for we might need the bedrooms for any female passengers before Paul is ready to travel. Right now, we need to get the coach to Buckboard on the road. Is breakfast almost ready? I'll send Ivan and Hank, and the passengers in for their meal. I'll take the water to Slim. Do you have an extra pot to spare? We can use the fireplace to heat water after this. Do you have bandages? We might need more."

"I'll tear up an old sheet, if you think more are needed. The porridge is ready, and Peter has gone to milk the nanny. Take

114

this water, son, while it's hot. Tell the men breakfast will be ready in a few minutes. Coffee's hot." Ruth grinned at her son. She knew his favorite expression to get the men moving in the mornings.

"Thanks, Mama. You're a jewel of great value." Joe grabbed a thick cloth, lifted the boiling water from the stove and carried it to the door. Ruth was two steps ahead of him, her arms full of clean cloths, soap and towels. They traipsed across the yard, with Joe careful not to spill the water on himself. She opened the door and left the cloths inside on a table in the hallway.

"Coming through with hot water," he yelled as he went down the hall. The place seemed to be filled with men. He came to the door where Slim was working over Paul and placed the pot on the table, and turned back into the hall. "Men, the food will be ready in about twenty minutes. Those of you riding on to Buckboard Station and Denver, get your belongings together. The stage will be leaving as soon as you eat."

Three of the men ducked into their rooms and came out with carpetbags and satchels and left for the house. The other man, Blandon, turned to Joe. "I can stay if you need me. I have no schedule to keep. You'll need an extra gun to make up a posse to go after the bandits. Or, I can help with the animals. I'm an experienced lawman. Wasn't much left of our town during the build-up to the war after the raiders came through. I've been rambling ever since; no home; no family."

Joe looked him in the eyes and believed his story. "I don't know what help you can be; I haven't thought out a plan, yet. You might better serve us if you go on to Denver and contact the authorities and tell them what happened; tell them to send some law officials here to investigate. These other fellows

115

might not tell the whole truth, maybe exaggerate. If you want to come back with the law, you'll be welcome. You noticed my Indian friend; he's a fine tracker. We may just follow the tracks and come back. I don't want anyone else hurt. If you'll take word to the stage line agent, see what he suggests we do; the stage's not due to run for another six days, so if you can do that for me, it would help considerable."

"I'll do that, Hadley. Give me a note for the officials and for the stage agent, so they'll know it's from you. I'll go on to Denver. Help where I can. I hope the young man makes it through the night. I've seen gunshot wounds before."

"Thanks, Blandon. For your information, so you'll know, I fought for the South; but I was regular army; we didn't engage in guerrilla warfare." Joe watched for a reaction and found one. The man stiffened, but then he relaxed.

Blandon held out his hand. "War's over, Hadley. The past is best forgotten by honest men."

"Thanks. Go get your breakfast before the coach leaves without you. I'll check my friend and make out those notes for you." Blandon went to his room and came out with a large carpetbag. Joe went to the room where Slim was working over Paul.

"How's he doing? Has he done any more talking?" He stood quietly in the doorway.

"No. I gave him some laudanum. He's in a great deal a pain. I got the bullet out and cauterized the skin. If there's no infection, he'll be alright." He turned to Joe. "I hate to hear about Manning. He was a strange man; always kept to himself. Quiet, but dangerous. Do you know if he had family?"

"No. He was from Ohio; fought in the Union Army. We spoke a few times, but like you say, he kept his private thoughts

116

to himself. I'll miss him. He was a good worker. I'll see the coach is on its way and come back so you can go eat." He shook his head. "Those men will probably start drinking at Buckboard, and by the time they reach Denver, the story will grow to enormous proportions. We'd best be prepared for an onslaught of strangers coming through out of curiosity. See you later."

Joe went to the coach. Ivan and Hank were looking at the exterior, Ivan in front, and Hank in the back putting away the dope pot. Joe went to each of the wheels and saw that the man had put extra grease on the axles. He opened the door and saw that the interior had been cleaned and dusted. He next went to the animals. It was a routine they carried out every time the coach left the station, but one that was more important today.

"Hank, one of the men is an experienced lawman; was in Missouri during the raids, name of Blandon. If you need help, call on him. Do you need an extra rifle or pistol? I hate to send you out like this. Those men may be waiting for you on the road. But, we need to continue the schedule if possible." He scraped his foot in the dirt, embarrassed to have to caution the men; they were experienced and loyal.

"We'll keep our eyes open, Joe. Don't fret yourself. What should we tell Weaver when we get there? Do you think these men will start drinking at Buckboard?"

"Yes. Damn, I always said Blessing should never have put that saloon in his station. I expect by the time the men get to Denver, the story will be spread over the Territory. We can expect a flood of curiosity seekers, newspaper men to come through. Tell Weaver as little as you can; the less the people know, the better it will be for us. God speed you on your way."

He left them and went in to eat his breakfast. It was bedlam

117

inside; men talking at once; the dog barking, the women serving the men food and drinks. He picked up the dog and put him in the inner garden. He reversed his steps and found paper and a pencil and wrote the notes for Tisdale and the law officials, whether local sheriff or Territorial lawmen. He sat in his place at the head of the table and tried to remain calm. Standing Tree was sitting in his usual location in front of the fireplace, his black eyes searching out each man with interest. Ruth poured Joe a cup of coffee, and he savored the taste and took a bite of ham. He took a biscuit from the basket and spread it with honey.

Ivan opened the door and yelled, "Ten minutes! Stage leaves in ten minutes." He shut the door. There was a scramble to finish their food, and a line formed at the outhouse. Hank came in for the beef jerky and biscuits for his and Ivan's satchels that Hannah always prepared for the trip. Joe took one more swallow and rose. He caught up with Blandon.

"I told the coachmen they could call on you, if they need help. Don't take action unless necessary. Ivan Mandrake's in charge of the animals and people. I trust him. You should, too." He handed the man his notes and shook hands.

The passengers climbed aboard, and the door was shut. Ivan and Hank finished putting the luggage in the rear boot and climbed into the box. Joe gave them a wave and they disappeared in the dimness of the forest road. He noticed that Slim had come to the door of the bunkhouse to see them off. Peter remained in the house. Joe needed some action to clear away the tenseness of the morning's activities. He found Standing Tree sitting under his tree, smoking his pipe.

"My friend, I don't know if you can understand what's happened. One of the stages was robbed and people killed. The man called Paul Ward was wounded. We need you to track to the stage and help us bury the dead, and see if we can find a trace of the men. There's a woman involved, and we should try to find her. Do you understand?"

The Indian nodded his understanding. "Men kill wagon. Woman gone. You want Standing Tree go; have look see, track varmints. Yes?"

"Yes. Get your bow and arrows, and your food bag; I'll saddle the horses; we may be gone all day; spend the night on the road. Watch out for bad white men."

He went to the bunkhouse and talked to Slim. He stayed while the man went to eat his meal, and when he returned he went to the house.

He took his son in his arms and held him a moment in the rocking chair; his baby smell was comforting after the trauma of the morning.

"Papa, I'm taking Standing Tree and following Paul's tracks to the coach, bury the dead if we can, and see where the bandit's tracks lead, then come back. Do you want to go? Slim has to stay with Paul, but we don't expect another coach for six days."

"No, son. I best stay with the women, at least until Ivan and Hank return. I'll keep a sharp lookout with my rifle at hand. I figure two, three days, when the news gets out, we'll be swamped with strangers. We need to get prepared. I'll bring in extra supplies from the shed: firewood and water. You do what you can for Manning and the others, but keep an eye open for trouble. Two men on horseback might not be noticed, but three will make dust that can be seen."

"Thanks, Papa. You always give good advice." He dug in his trunk for his old army canteen, took the bag of food Hannah prepared, kissed her on the cheek and gave his mother a hug.

"Don't forget to let Jack out of the garden. He's probably dug up all the flowers by now." He laughed at the expressions on their faces.

He went to the barn and saddled Mack, his personal mount, and chose a sorrel stallion for Standing Tree. The Indian didn't use a saddle, only a wool blanket. He was ready to go; his bow and quiver hung over his shoulder, his medicine bag around his neck, his food bag around his waist and his knife at his hip.

It was shortly before noon when they left the station and followed Paul's tracks south. They wobbled at first, indicating his weakness and stumbling gait; but quickened as they neared the stage. Standing Tree pointed to some buzzards circling in the sky overhead, and they knew they were close. They found the wreckage among some boulders and scrub bushes. The tracks indicated the bandits had lain in wait. There were a few sulfur matches and cigar butts on the ground; rifle shells and damp spots with brown indentions where one of the men spat his tobacco. The Indian held up five fingers, and Joe knew that meant five men.

The bodies were strewn about, and Joe had to use his jacket to scare the birds away. The ants and insects had begun their work. One passenger was lying inside the coach; the other a few feet away. Manning had given a good fight from the amount of shells from his shotgun lying beside the front boot and scattered across the ground around the coach. He must have jumped or was slung from the coach when it went over, and then he had used it for protection. Joe climbed inside the coach, and with the Indian's help lifted the first passenger out. They laid him on the ground, stretched out the second body and carried Manning to their side. Joe found a flat area under a scrawny pine and started digging the pit. Standing Tree kept watch for men and birds while he worked. He began to sweat profusely in the sunshine.

He took a short break for a drink of water and began again. The Indian called to him, and he looked up. The birds were circling again. The Indian took the shovel and signed for him to rest and watch. He walked some distance away and examined the ground carefully. He considered whether he should take the personal effects from the bodies or leave them. Important papers or credentials might help with the investigation the stage line would surely do. He looked through the pockets but finally decided that to remove anything would be disrespectful. Once he was finished, he delved into the boot to check the contents. He took out his small tablet and pencil and wrote down a description of everything he found, and had Standing Tree make his mark. An Indian's view might not stand up in a court of law, but at least he was a witness.

They lowered the bodies into the pit and covered it with dirt and rocks. There was nothing else to be done for them. He made a drawing of the position of the coach to the rocks and shrubs and the distant mountains that could be seen on the horizon. He was reminded of the first day he saw the mountains and his excitement. He sighed with sadness, said a short prayer over the pit and he and the Indian mounted the horses to start tracking. He was careful not to disturb the original tracks. He could make out the tracks of several horses, confirming what he'd been told, and the tracks of a woman or small child being led by a rope or chain. He was so angry, he had to stop and calm himself.

They followed the tracks for about three miles until the ground became more broken and jagged rocks appeared. There were shallow gullies and dried creek beds with a few scrub bushes and creosote shrubs. Here and there was a cedar or juniper tree, as well as a few scraggly pines, stunted in growth. They stopped to eat and drink some water, and Joe drew a picture of the landscape. They rode about two more miles and noticed the birds were circling again about fifty yards away. The tracks led directly to a long shallow dried creek bed or ravine, with a line of willow trees along its rim. Joe was no expert, but he fancied there was water underneath the bed, or the trees wouldn't be so green and healthy. He dismounted and walked down the center of the bed, while Standing Tree walked the horses and kept watch. After about twenty yards he saw a multitude of tracks, and under a bush he found the body of the woman.

It was obvious even to his untrained eyes that she'd been raped, tortured and abused. She was lying half-naked, her legs and lower torso exposed to the elements. The bodice of her dress was ripped open, and knife marks covered her breasts; her blonde hair was matted, and dried blood caked with dirt encircled her face. Joe didn't see any bullet marks, so he wasn't sure what had caused her death, perhaps exposure in the night cold and damp. He rose out of the gully, dug a hole and buried her under a scrawny willow tree. He made a mark on the tree for the officials when they came to investigate if they did come. They marked the tracks headed north-northwest toward Denver. He made notes in his tablet, and he and Standing Tree headed home. There was nothing more he could do but pray for the souls who had departed this life in such a tragic manner.

They rode through the late afternoon and stopped to camp not far from the wreckage of the coach. Joe took the first watch, for he was exhausted in mind, body and spirit, and couldn't rest. Standing Tee woke him just before sunrise. The air was damp and chilly, and he was cold to the bones, but they dared not make a fire. They rode in silence, each wrapped in his own thoughts. Once again, they found and followed Paul's tracks and arrived about mid-morning. Joe made note of the date in his tablet.

The station appeared quiet as they approached, but Joe heard the barking of a dog, and knew the sound of Jack's alarm. They slowed their approach, but all was well. Peter came out to greet them, his rifle in the crook of his arm. There was a wagon in the open space near the spring, and several horses tied to the trees. Joe groaned. The human vultures and sight-seekers had arrived.

Eleven

"Hello, son. Was your trip successful?"

Joe could tell from the expression on his father's face that he was tense and frustrated. The question seemed odd; and he glanced around to see what made him so. Standing on the porch was a man in a dark blue shirt and trousers. There was something shiny on his chest; a lawman, probably the sheriff. Or, maybe a federal marshal.

"Yes, and no, Papa. We found the coach and bodies, but not the bandits. Who's here?" Joe stepped down from his horse, working his rifle scabbard from the horn of his saddle and onto his shoulder.

"Damn lawmen, snooping around here, instead of out doing what you were doing, looking for clues to the robbery. Came early this morning and asked a hundred questions, like we had something to do with it. Had Ruth in tears once. Here, let me take care of the horses. I need some release from my frustration." Peter handed Joe his rifle and took the reins of the horses to lead them to the fence, where he could groom them and put them in their stalls.

"Is Paul still with us?"

"Yes, Slim's watching him. Had a fever and talking out of his head, but Slim says he'll soon be on the mend. That passenger, Blandon? He came back with the marshal. Has a letter from Tisdale; said he'd be here tomorrow. Go get something to eat, boy. You need some rest. Not that you'll get any with that man here."

"Thanks, Papa." Joe turned to Standing Tree and signed for him to follow, as he made his way to the house, carrying his father's rifle in one arm and his burlap bag in the other. His own rifle in its scabbard bumped his hip as he walked.

"Are you Hadley?" the man with the shiny badge asked. He was of average height, with long side hair along his cheeks and a heavy mustache. He looked to be in his thirties, had piercing gray eyes under his broad-brimmed hat and a lethal-looking gun on his hip.

"Yes, I'm Joe Hadley. That was my father I was just talking to back there." Joe smiled, but the man wasn't amused.

"Been waitin' for ya. Blandon says you're the one in charge of this station. Said you'd gone to the site of the tragedy. What'd ya find? Who's that Injun with ya?"

"This is my Arapahoe tracker friend and big game hunter. His name's Standing Tree. Been with us for three years; saved us from starvation several times. If you'll wait until I greet my wife and mother, and check on my friends, I'll tell you what you want to know. Have you had dinner?" Joe knew he was telling a big white lie, for the supplies from Tisdale came regularly since he had taken the job from Baldwin, the Eastern Agent.

"Yes. Your wife gave us some beans and cornpone when we arrived. I brought several men with me. That's their horses and wagon near the spring. You take your time. I'll help my deputies set up camp under the trees. Your father said it was a good spot. We brought a tent and supplies with us." Surprisingly, he seemed to mellow when he heard the description of Standing Tree, and now he stuck out his hand and shook Joe's, with a smile. "Name's Captain Sizemore."

"I'll see you later, then." Joe was puzzled. Why had his father said the man was hostile and gruff? He seemed to be a pleasant fellow, only doing his job. He entered the house and saw Hannah at the stove. Ruth sat near the fireplace tending the child. Standing Tree went to the table and sat down. Joe put the two rifles on the high shelf beside the fireplace. He put his bag on the table and kissed Hannah on the cheek. He waved at his mother and got a wave in return.

"Hello, darling. Is all well?" Joe looked around the room to see if anything was out of place, but it was the same as when he left.

"Oh, Joe. I'm glad you're back. That deputy, Browning, is driving us to distraction, with his questions and penetrating looks, as though Ruth and I know anything about the bandits. Did you find the coach?"

"Browning? I just met a Sizemore. Should I know this Browning?"

"No, I suppose not." Hannah was terse, and Joe knew it was her frustration coming through. "The captain has been well-mannered and polite. His deputy has not. Tell me what you discovered."

"Yes. We found the coach and the woman." Joe could see that his wife was tired. He wished he could help her, but he didn't know much about cooking food. "It was bad; we buried them, and followed the tracks for some fifty yards. They seem

126

to be heading to Denver or maybe west of there into the mountains. I hope everything is alright at Rockland Station; the tracks led in that direction. I wish there was some way to get the information to Moore and his wife to watch for trouble. I'll be glad when the telegraph wires are up this way. Now for the important news. I'm hungry."

"Well, of course you are. Sit down, dear." She turned to get a cup and the coffee pot. As soon as she poured him a steaming cup of the dark brown brew, she lifted the pot of beans onto the table and a basket of johnnycakes. She gave Standing Tree a glass of water, who always refused coffee because he didn't care for the taste of it. She gave him a smile, and he looked at her.

"Scarred Woman good cook. Think better than Yo Hadley, maybe."

"Why, thank you. I'm sure you've grown tired of stale biscuits and beef jerky. I'll fry up some sausage, and there's pie left." She turned to the stove to suit her actions to her words.

Joe dipped a large portion of beans onto his plate for himself and filled his friend's plate; and they started eating, while the aroma of cooking sausage filled the air. He reached for an onion and cut it into small pieces and threw them into his beans. He asked his friend silently if he wanted some onion, but he shook his head.

Around the side of a mouth stuffed with beans, Joe asked, "What kind of questions has Browning been asking?"

"Oh," Hannah began, as she flipped the sausage over with a large spoon and turned, "he wanted to know how often the stage comes from the south; who drives it; have we had trouble before? How many passengers come through; do they stay overnight; where are they going? He wanted to know about

127

Paul and Manning. That sort of thing. But Ruth and I don't know the answers. We told him to wait until you get back. You're the manager. Papa told him as much as he knew, which isn't any more than us. He talked to Ivan and Hank and Slim, but Paul's still asleep. He had a terrible time the first night. Crying out in the fever; Slim kept him quiet with the laudanum." The sausage was done, and she lifted a couple of pieces from the skillet to his plate and gave the rest to Standing Tree, who grunted his thanks.

Joe finished his meal. "Can you put some water on for bathing? I'm ripe. I'll find us some clean clothes. It's a warm day, so might be nice to bathe in the garden. Too many people around the place outside, or I'd take a dip in the creek." He motioned for Standing Tree to stay until he was ready for him. He went to the bedroom and chose two shirts and two pairs of trousers. The Indian saw no need for undergarments, so Joe picked out some long handles and clean socks for himself. He grabbed a couple of flannel towels, soap and his razor. He went outside for the large tub used for baths and clothes washing and took it to the inner garden. When all was ready, he lifted the pot of hot water and dumped it into the tub. It felt good to relax in the tub for a moment, away from the turmoil and with the blue sky above him; but he had chores to do, so he finished and dressed.

He went in and took more hot water to the tub and signed for the Indian to take his bath. The Indian would have much preferred the creek, Joe was certain, but with so many strangers stirring around, Joe didn't want him embarrassed. He left him to his bath and went in to visit with his mother and his child. When Standing Tree came back, in fresh clothes and his hair neatly braided, Joe emptied the tub and hung it back on the wall.

Fortified with food and clean clothes, Joe left the Indian under his tree, smoking his pipe, and went to the bunkhouse to check on Paul.

The door was open to the room. Paul was asleep and alone, so he left and went to the barn, where he found Slim with a mule.

"Hello. Got a problem?"

Slim jumped with nervousness, and turned. "There you are, Joe, I'm glad you're back. Those men are driving me daft. Questions. Questions. I answered as much as I could, but I'm only the animal handler. I don't know anything about the business. I kept mum about the railroad coming through." He frowned. "This stubborn mule broke away from the herd and got out of the corral. Knocked two logs off the top of the fence and as a result has a cut on his leg. I've put salve on it and a bandage, and he needs to be kept off it for a while, but he won't lie down. Sometimes, my friend, I'd like to go off like you did and leave it all behind me."

"Truly? Well, as soon as this business about the holdup is over, maybe you can take a trip to Denver for some relaxation. How is Paul?" He frowned as he looked around. The place wasn't as neat as usual; bottles were out of place; his surgery tools exposed to the air and germs. It wasn't like Slim to be so careless.

"He's healing fast; no sign of infection. Had a bad fever the first night, but has calmed down. He's been sleeping. He'll be able to drive the coach again in a couple of months, if he doesn't let his arm grow stiff from not exercising it. There's the temptation to not move a limb when it hurts to do so. How was your trip?" As he was talking, Slim began to put away bottles, and placed his tools in a pan for washing. Joe felt better.

Perhaps the man was just too busy. They left the mule and strolled from the surgery section to the outside, where they could talk.

They squatted near the door and watched the activity at the lawmen's camp. Joe began to describe what he had found and asked what had happened while he was gone from the station.

"Where are Ivan and Hank?" Joe looked around him, thinking he might see them.

"They took off on saddle horses for the river to do some fishing. I suspect they wanted to get away from the lawmen. The stage comes tomorrow, and some fish sounds like a good change of diet. I'd go myself if there wasn't Paul to look after. That's one strong man; got a lot of courage, too, to walk for help after what he went through."

"Has he spoken at all while I was gone?"

"No, I've kept him sedated until he gets his strength back. There's time enough for that."

"Slim, as soon as the men get back from their fishing, you take some time to rest. I'll watch Paul for you and see to the coaches tomorrow. If you can't go fishing, then at least lie down in your room with the door locked. I suspect the marshal will want me to go back to the coach with him, and I'll have to go, but at least I'd like to wait until the stages come through. I'll talk to Blandon. He said he could help with the animals. Have you talked with him?"

"Blandon? No. Is he the passenger on the stage from Denver? I supposed he'd go with the marshal; they've been pretty chummy since he came back with them this morning. Who is he?"

"He told me he was a lawman in Missouri; got wiped out by the raiders and came west to find a job." He frowned.

"Maybe I should talk to him again, alone. Damn, Slim. Why did those bandits choose to come into our space to cause havoc? Well, I best go speak with the marshal, tell him what I found. You take a nap, relax. We'll take over until supper. Lock your door."

"Thanks, Joe. Watch that mule, will you? Put on a clean poultice if it needs one. Peter will know what to do." Slim got up and went to the bunkhouse. Joe sighed and rose to meet with the lawmen. He'd like to take a nap, too. He walked to the lawman's camp. He saw maybe twelve men sitting or standing under the trees. One of them was tending a small fire in a pit, surrounded by rocks. He was glad to see they'd taken precautions against a forest fire.

"Captain Sizemore? Can we have that talk now? I have to start getting ready for the stages coming in from the east and south tomorrow. We have a sick man, and the animals need attention." He took his tablet from his pocket. "I took notes of what I saw. We buried the victims, the girl, too. We didn't take anything off them, but I made a note of what was in their pockets." Joe stopped talking at the shock on the man's face.

"There was a woman involved? No one said anything about a woman. Blandon," he yelled. Joe saw the man rise from his position under a large Ponderosa pine and come forward. He looked like he hadn't slept in days; his clothes were rumpled and one button was missing from his coat.

"Blandon, Hadley says there was a woman involved. Why the hell didn't you tell me that?"

"Captain, I figured to wait for Hadley to come back. Wouldn't have helped the poor soul, me telling you about her." He looked keenly at Joe, his eyes alert. "Did you find her?"

"Yes. We found her. We buried her and put a mark on a tree

so you can find the grave, if you need to exhume the body for clues to the mystery. She was in bad shape, tortured, raped, I think, cut on the breast with a knife." He looked to the far distant mountains to keep from being sick.

"Well, we won't disturb her, then. She's suffered enough. Tell me about the others. What kind of shape was the coach? Can it be saved?" The three men stood under the shade of a large cottonwood, and for the better part of an hour, Joe told all he knew. He brought out his tablet and showed them his diagrams and notes. He tore out the pages and gave them to Sizemore.

A tall, burly, clean-shaven man came to join them, and Sizemore introduced him as Platt Browning. Joe now knew the cause of his father's irritation and his wife's distress, as the deputy repeatedly interrupted Sizemore with his questions. He seemed to have a nervous tick in one eye, as he had to blink often. He took a handkerchief from his pocket and wiped his watery eyes. Joe stepped back when the man got into his face and said, "Where'd you bury the woman?" Joe looked to Sizemore, but he was gazing at the distant mountains, and Joe was curious as to who was actually in charge.

It was decided the Captain and his men would start early the next morning with his supply wagon to investigate the crime scene. Joe suggested they leave the wagon and take a couple of the station's mules, instead. The captain looked sharply at Joe and agreed, it might be the better course, since a wagon might attract attention. In spite of the sight of the tracks moving toward Rockland Station, the raiders could still be in the neighborhood, or have circled back toward the south.

They shook hands, and the captain promised to return to Sweetwater when he finished his work.

Joe strode toward the house, and Blandon walked beside him. He was silent at first; then stopped and looked around to see if anyone was near.

"Hadley, I have a letter from Tisdale. He's coming on a special stage tomorrow, not the regular run. Bringing his wife so she can visit your family. Said it'll look more friendly that way. I tried to talk him out of it; the bandits may be on the trail; and you've confirmed they were headed toward Rockland, but he was adamant. Mrs. Tisdale knows the danger, he said. But, they have to get the stage line back to some semblance of order, or the people will stop riding, he said. I didn't say anything to the captain or your people. Waited to talk to you." He took the letter from his vest pocket and handed it to Joe.

Joe took it and glanced at the address on the front which said simply, "Joe Hadley." It was so like Tisdale to insist his wife come with him. He put the letter in his own pocket and started toward the house again. "Blandon, is that offer of yours to help still good?" He looked at the mountains again.

"You want me to deliver another message?" Blandon glanced at Joe.

"No. I need help here. My animal handler is already exhausted from caring for the stage driver and the animals. He needs a break. My father's in a sweat over the way the lawmen treated my mother; me, too, for that matter, but I understand their need to ask questions. The two coachmen may have to make an extra run or two either to Buckboard Station on the west or Mozier on the east. It looks like we're going to have a lot of company in the next few days as the news spreads wider. It's probably already in the Denver papers. I need help with the business end." He gazed at Blandon with a droll expression. "Might need you to take secret messages for Tisdale." He smiled.

"I gotcha. I know how to shoe horses and plow a field, though I haven't done it in a few years."

"Ever milked a goat?" Joe continued to the house.

"No, can't say I have. Milked a cow though, growing up. We didn't have a large farm, but had a milk cow and chickens. We had some tame rabbits, too. I haven't had rabbit meat in a long while. I heard your men went off fishing this morning. Where's this fishing place? I like to fish." With a few casual words, the bond was forged and understood. Blandon was to work for Joe until the matter of the stage robbery was settled, and do a little spying on the side if necessary.

Joe stopped at the front porch. "Put your things in one of the empty rooms in the bunkhouse. Thanks." He shook his hand and turned into the house.

A whirlwind on two legs met him as he entered. Beside the boy was a dog, barking a welcome.

"Papa. Papa. Up. Up."

Joe picked up the boy and threw him high in the air, then lowered him and hugged him tight. The boy squirmed to get down, laughing. The dog ran circles around his tail. Ruth stood nearby with a surprised twinkle in her eyes and spoke sharply to the dog. He quieted down and went to his place in front of the fireplace, but his eyes stayed alert. Hannah was at the stove with an oversized spoon, stirring something in a large pot. Standing Tree was sitting in his place, his black eyes on Joe, waiting for a signal to join him, but Joe went to him, instead.

He spoke to the Indian in a low voice, while he watched Ruth guide the boy to the table and give him a piece of bread soaked in milk.

"The white men are going to the wrecked coach tomorrow.

134

They need a tracker, someone familiar with the place. Will you go?"

"Yo Hadley go?"

"No." He shook his head and made the negative sign in the Indian medium.

"Yo Hadley want Standing Tree go with white men?"

"Yes. They need you. Show where men buried; show where white woman buried beside ravine."

Standing Tree looked at the boy at the table, and at Hannah and Ruth, and said, "Come." He rose from his spot on the floor and went out the door. Joe signed to Hannah that he was going out; he plucked his hat from the peg by the door and followed Standing Tree.

They moved deep into the forest, about twenty-five yards, before Standing Tree stopped.

"Yo Hadley sit. I talk."

Joe squatted on the ground under a majestic Ponderosa pine tree. He looked to his Indian friend. He was bewildered. What could it mean?

The Indian filled his pipe with tobacco and began to smoke. He squatted beside Joe. He blew smoke to the north, the south, the east and then the west. His eyes were watering from the exercise.

"Many moon past, before white soldiers come to fort at two rivers, old man called Lone Deer speak to Big Father in Sky in a dream; he tell small boy his dream. Small boy, Standing Tree, grandson, me. Lone Deer say in dream some day in far distance place Standing Tree find home among white people. Standing Tree not believe. He warrior like father, Wolf Killer, die in battle with Crow village. Standing Tree raised in American school by mighty river Ar-kan-sa. Grow up; go home to village.

Forget dream of grandfather. Kill many enemies, Crow, Black Feet, Sioux. Marry Face in Moon, have boy child."

Joe waited patiently for the Indian to go on with his tale. His legs ached, and he changed positions. Standing Tree glanced at him and took a few puffs on his pipe. Joe sat flat on the ground. He looked around at the trees and bushes. A ground squirrel chattered among the boulders. He saw some ants marching in a line across a bed of pine needles and leaves. Standing Tree started to speak, and Joe looked up.

"Face in Moon dead. Child dead. Fever of white man. Standing Tree hate white man. Want war with white man. War with white soldiers at fort. Go on raids, kill, burn house of white man."

Joe felt sick, but he didn't let any expression form on his face. He waited for the finish, his heart pounding and pulse racing.

"Standing Tree now old man like grandfather Lone Deer. Many moon pass by. He have dream in forest; time soon come join Big Father in Sky. He speak to village elders. They say, 'Go.' No family; no sons, no woman to cook for Standing Tree. He go. Walk far distance; big storm come; hide in cave; large stones fall from sky; wait to die. Hungry. Belly hurt. No die. Standing Tree see smoke in chim-nee. Walk to smoke. White man house. Tired. Need sleep. Wake in dark; see Scarred Woman come to little house in back. Standing Tree keep still. White Man come with long gun. Standing Tree wait to die, but no die. White Man give food, water, smile on face. Shake hand with Injun. Apache woman, Apache boy, Sammie in house. Yo Hadley my friend. Save life of Standing Tree; make big medicine, take on horse hunt; deer hunt. No more Standing Tree old, forgotten by Big Father in Sky. Live free. No war." The

Indian emptied his pipe and put it in his trousers' pocket. He reached for the pouch hanging from a leather strap around his neck.

He opened it and showed Joe a dried root of some sort, a small feather and a turquoise stone the size of his fingernail. He said, "Earth, sky, water stone. Standing Tree no longer hate white man. Now, evil ones come to white man friends of Standing Tree, white woman. Standing Tree go with man with shiny metal on chest." He placed the objects back in the pouch and handed it to Joe.

"If Standing Tree no come back, Yo Hadey give to small boy child. Teach about Lone Deer and Dream Come True; tell of Wolf Killer, my father; tell of Face in Moon; Arapahoe people gone from land. You do this for friend Standing Tree?"

Joe stood and with a solemn face said, "I will." They shook hands and turned back for the station. Joe was quivering with his reaction. In all his young life, he had never had such a friend, and his heart thundered in his chest cavity; his breath came short and shallow as though he had run a mile. They didn't speak when they came in sight of the house. Standing Tree went to sit in his usual place, his eyes taking in the action.

Joe moved on to the barn where he went from stall to stall, checking the saddle horses. He selected six horses for the westbound stage and six mules for the eastern stage and put them in the holding pen. Ivan and Hank were back, and he spent some time filling them in on what he had found. They could only wait to see what the morrow brought. He went to Slim's room, but the door was locked, and he went to see Paul. The man was awake.

"Hello. Glad to see you're back with us. Has the marshal been to see you?" He sat beside the bed.

"Yes. Would you get me a drink of water, Joe? Where's Slim?" Paul tried to sit up but grimaced in pain, and Joe rose to pour some water from the pitcher into a glass and helped the man drink.

"He's taking some time off. The stage from Mozier's station is due tomorrow, and likewise Owens' northbound coach from Trinidad, if there are passengers. How do you feel?"

"Like hell. Like I been kicked by one of your mules. How the hell do you think I feel?" He took another sip of water and coughed. "Did you find her? Did you find the woman?" He finished the water and gave Joe the glass.

"Yes, we found her. We buried her where she fell. We buried Manning and the two passengers, too. The rest is in the hands of the law. I did all I could. Life goes on. Have you thought about what you'll do? You can stay here as long as you need to. Tisdale should be here tomorrow. He's coming on a special stage and bringing his wife with him." He was interrupted with a string of curses.

"Damn, Joe. Has the man no sense? To bring his wife from Denver with the highway men on the loose. He should know better."

"He knows the danger. And, Betty does, too. He's willing to take the risk, for if the stage stops bringing women, we'll lose business. With the threat from the railroads north of here, we can't afford to lose the customers we have." He looked around the room. "Do you need anything? Some food, maybe?"

"Sure, bring me a big piece of venison, with Hannah's apple pie for dessert. And, coffee. Lots of coffee." His eyes twinkled with an inner spirit. "Tell Ruth I could use some of her fried eggs if any are available." He reached out his hand and sobered. Joe shook his hand. "Thanks, Joe, for the offer. I'll see what

Tisdale says. He might have a place for me somewhere else on the line; or the coach may be repaired, and I can make the same run."

"Good-night, Paul. Rest easy. I'll send someone with some food." He glanced at Slim's door as he passed it in the hallway, but it was still closed. He went to check on the injured mule, and changed the poultice. He took a harness from the barn, tossed it over his shoulder and marched to the house. The harnesses needed constant care, and it would give him something to do with his hands.

Twelve

The table was filled that night. The captain was there, his deputy Platt Browning and Hawk Blandon. Standing Tree ate in his usual place. Hank took some soup, fried fish and apple pie to the bunkhouse for Paul, with a pot of coffee. He laughed when he sat down.

"Paul said he'd rather have a big venison steak, but fish would have to do. He said to tell you thanks for the pie. Slim finally woke up and was with him. He'll be here in a while, after he sees to that mule that broke down the fence." He dipped into the soup, filled his bowl and commenced to eat.

The conversation centered on politics and local things, until Standing Tree stood and gathered his blanket around his shoulders. He spoke in his deep voice. Everyone looked up and stopped eating.

"Yo Hadley say I go with man with shiny metal on chest to find tracks of evil ones who kill white woman. I go. Good fish. Better pie. Scarred Woman fine cook, I think." He left them in his usual dignified manner. The strangers watched him go with speculation in their eyes, but Joe and the others continued eating.

"Where'd that Injun come from, Hadley? He seems to have acquired a good education in the white man's language. Arapahoe, you said? Is he a good tracker?" The captain cut a small piece of fish and fit it in his mouth and chewed.

"I don't know exactly where his tribe first settled, but he came from somewhere in the area of Fort Laramie. Went to school at some mission in Arkansas. Got lost in a heavy hail storm we had a few years back and came toward the smoke in the chimney. Been with us ever since. He's a good tracker; he knows where we found the coach and men. You can trust him, as long as you treat him with the respect he deserves." He gave the captain and deputy such a fierce glare that they knew he meant his words. He continued eating and sat back from the table. "That was fine, darling. Ivan, I need to talk to you and Hank. I'll see you at the corrals. Papa, you stay here. I'll be back soon." He left the house, his rifle in his arm, his hat on his head and his coat buttoned to his neck.

As he paused on the porch, he watched the men walking to and fro in the camp by the spring. Someone had set up a large tent. When he heard a noise behind him, he walked toward the corrals, his ears alert to the night sounds. It was a warm night, the air still and the smell of wood smoke in his nostrils. The faint scent of blooming flowers and pine mingled with the smoke. He took a deep breath and sensed the presence of the men behind him. He turned to greet them.

"Tisdale will be here tomorrow at some time. I figure if he leaves Rockland before dawn he'll be here by afternoon. He'll determine what's to be done, but I fancy he'll change the route from the south, Paul's route. If the coach can be raised and repaired it'll take weeks, maybe months. It'll be at least that

141

long before Paul is able to drive again. The two of you'll have to take up some of the slack. We'll see what he says. He may even transfer you to Trinidad or Pueblo. What with the railroad almost finished from Wyoming to Utah, the east-west route may be eliminated altogether. Before he gets here, I want to thank you personally for your service and loyalty. I'll stay here whatever Tisdale says. This is my home, and I can't pull up stakes and move my parents again. I've talked to Blandon, and he's agreed to help with the work of the station. Slim may be transferred to another station, or he might decide to open an office in Denver. Things will change because of this hold-up. Nothing will be as it was again."

"Hell, Joe. What are you saying? You think Tisdale will shut down Sweetwater and Mozier? I wouldn't mind driving south but, I hate those high mountain passes and deep valleys. It puts a strain on a man's mind and arms. What do you think, Hank?"

"I'll do what Tisdale wants me to do. We been reading about the bandits in Missouri and Nebraska, other places east of here, but I never thought they'd try it. It puts a fright into a man's heart to think of what happened to Manning, and he was a good man, a dead shot with his gun. But, I knew the dangers involved when I took the job. I'll stick with the stage line until the end."

"Good man. Well, I'm going to talk with Slim. Check the saddle horses; they had a long trip, and hit the bed. I'll see you early in the morning." He strode to the bunkhouse, followed by the two men. They separated at the door. They went to their rooms and shut the doors. He continued to Slim's room and knocked. He wasn't there, so he went to the barn and checked on Mack and the sorrel that Standing Tree had ridden.

142

When Joe came in, the dog rose and wagged his tail. Joe gave him a scratch under the chin, and the animal moved back to his place and plopped down before the fire. Joe removed his hat and coat and hung them on the pegs by the door. He placed his rifle on the high shelf and sat down with a sigh.

Hannah gave him a glass of water. The coffee pot was empty. He drank most of the liquid and put down the glass. Slim was eating his supper. Ruth had put the boy to bed and gone herself. Hannah was putting beans in a pot to soak overnight. Peter sat in the rocking chair.

Slim spoke around the food in his mouth. "I talked with the man called Blandon. He said you'd asked him to stay. Joe, I can do the work. I was just tired and out of sorts. I feel rested now." He seemed upset.

"I know you can do the work. I expect you to continue, but I'm not sure how this robbery has changed things. Tisdale will be here tomorrow with his wife." Hannah gasped and sat down. Joe gave her a slight grin of apology. "I think he'll change the routes. With the talk of the railroad, and now the stoppage of the route from Pueblo, he may have that routed through here, or he may shut down Mozier altogether. We may have two stages a week from the south. Mozier's been a north-south artery since the beginning." He sighed. "I don't know where we'll put the females if we have more coming through. I'm sorry, dear; I've been trying to think this through. We can double up in the bunkhouse with the single men, but we only have two rooms in the house. I might have to set up another tent." He looked at Hannah and laughed. She smiled.

"Do you think he'll do that? Shut down Mozier? Where will Youngblood and his wife go?"

"I don't know." He looked up when Peter came to stand

143

beside the table.

"Well, it won't do to sit up all night speculating on what will or won't happen. I'm going to bed. I'll take the early morning shift at guard, although with all these lawmen around, I think we're safe enough." He laughed and went toward the hallway.

"What will you do, if they shut down Sweetwater?" Slim shoved his plate and utensils aside. Hannah took them to the wash pan and put them in; she didn't wash them, but came back to sit down.

"We'll stay here. This is my home. I figure the north-south route will continue for a few more years, until someone builds the railroad. Time enough to decide what to do then." He took Hannah's hand in his and smiled.

"Oh. Well, I guess I'd better leave you. I slept all afternoon, so I'm not sleepy. I'll check on Paul and maybe find someone up at the lawman's camp. If not, I'll keep a lookout for a few hours, and let you sleep. I have some thinking to do. Goodnight."

Joe and Hannah sat for a while longer, silently contemplating how their lives had changed. She rose and finished washing the dishes and went to the bedroom. Joe gazed into the burning coals of the fireplace for a long time, and made sure there was no danger of fire. He didn't rest well and woke in the midst of a nightmare. He sat up in a panic.

"Joe?"

He couldn't see Hannah clearly, only a shadowy figure among the whiteness of the bedclothes. He leaned over and kissed her on the head. "Shush, go back to sleep. I'm fine." She snuggled down and he covered her with the quilt.

He lay beside her, his mind a jumble of almost forgotten

people of the past; the meeting in the forest with Standing Tree; the present troubles and the picture of the woman as they had found her in the ravine. He suddenly remembered Tisdale's letter, rose and dressed in his trousers and threw a blanket around his shoulders.

He lit a lamp in the kitchen, and Jack, the dog, jerked awake and went to the door and stood whining until Joe let him out. He quickly returned, and Joe closed and locked the door behind him. Jack flopped on the floor and soon was asleep, and Joe sat at the small table Hannah used for cooking.

"Hadley, I'm coming by special stage for a visit and bringing Betty with me. It's imperative that we keep up appearances at this time of tumult. She realizes the danger, but is determined to come and visit with Hannah and Ruth. I received your message by way of Blandon and he seems a capable man; I'll see if I can find him a position with the stage line. He tells me he has no responsibilities to hold him elsewhere. I'm bringing with me an experienced wheelwright and blacksmith to determine if the coach can be righted and repaired. We need your continued assistance in this matter. The law has been informed of the tragedy and should have reached the station by the time I'm able to travel. I look forward to seeing you again in your home. Wallace Tisdale, Western Division Agent, Overland Stage and Mail Service."

The last line drew his attention, and Joe wanted to shout with joy. They had won the mail contract for the southern and western route. Then he groaned, because it meant more responsibility, as he would have the United States government to deal with in getting the mail bags through safely and on time. He folded the letter, put it between the pages of the Bible and sat in the rocking chair in the semi-darkness. His head ached, and his belly felt empty.

His thoughts drifted from stage business to the trip into the forest with Standing Tree. He realized with a sinking heart the significance of the talk. His Indian friend was telling him good-bye. He didn't expect to survive the trip. An overwhelming urge to get on his knees came, and he resisted for a while, but it persisted, and he obeyed. He prayed earnestly for the safety of his friend, the future of the stage line and his family. A coal fell in the fireplace with a thunk, and he felt it was a sign. He rose and went to bed, snuggled against the warm body of his wife and fell into a peaceful asleep.

Thirteen

The next morning, the station was a beehive of activity. Before the day at the station got truly started, Captain Sizemore, with Standing Tree leading the way on a bay stallion, his bow and quiver of arrows on his back, his food bag full of treats given to him by Hannah, and the other men trailing behind with a mule packed with supplies, headed south to follow the tracks of Paul Ward to the wrecked coach. Their supply wagon remained parked under the pine trees near the spring.

Closer to home, Peter went about the yard, doing his chores as usual, taking care of the nanny and the chickens. Hannah and Ruth cooked breakfast for the station's residents, and they also went about their usual tasks. Ivan drove the black coach into the yard for service in the usual manner and unhitched the horses, for Joe didn't know whether it would require horses or mules. He had teams of each selected: one of mules for Rusty's big brown coach, a team of horses for Ivan to use, as well as one for Jim Owens' coach if it came from Trinidad as per schedule.

Paul was able, with the help of Slim, to walk to the house and eat a full breakfast. He strolled around the station a bit then went back to bed and slept the rest of the morning.

Slim declared the mule well enough to be put back in the corral, and hammered away at the forge preparing for the onslaught of visitors. Ivan and Hank whiled away the extra time getting their gear together and cleaning the coach's interior. Blandon, at the behest of Slim, cleaned the barn and gave the saddle horses fresh hay and grain. Joe lit a pit fire to help the ladies wash the clothes. The bed sheets and clothing were flapping in the brisk breeze from the south, when the first wagon arrived. It was accompanied by six men on horseback.

A flaccid, pale faced man with a full beard named Rolf Livingston dropped from the wagon, walked up to Hank and demanded to talk with the manager. Hank pointed to Joe and went on with his work. Finished with the interior, the coachmen checked the wheels and the rear boot and front boot for cracks and cuts in the leather or wood. Ivan called on Hannah's service, and she repaired a small cut with her needle and thread. Ruth watched over Fuller and the dog.

Livingston was found to be from the Denver newspaper, wanting news of the robbery. Joe told him what he thought appropriate and directed him to the law officials for more. The men on horseback gained as much information as they cared for and took off at a trot for the wreckage, the newsman's wagon following more slowly.

Smoke curled from the stove chimney and the fireplace. The air was ripe with the odor of dust, wood smoke and manure from the barn that Blandon had dumped to be used in the fields when it dried. The sound of wheels came in an echo from the forest as Rance Potter, with a great bellow and a cloud of dust, stopped the red coach with the black trim within steps of the cottonwood trees beside the creek. He jumped down from the box and ran at a clip to Joe and gave him a big hug.

Astonished, Joe dropped the ax he had been using to chop firewood and laughed until his sides hurt. More slowly and with less enthusiasm Thad Ray shook his hand. From the coach with the grace of a Madonna emerged Betty Tisdale and her children, Mariah and Jeff. She was followed by the man whom they had been expecting, the Boss, Wallace Tisdale, Western Division Agent. A short, dumpy fellow with a goatee and mustache detached himself from the crowd and started walking around. Joe watched him and decided he couldn't be the wheelwright and blacksmith; he was too small. He heard a sound, and lastly stepping from the coach was a giant, a man over six feet tall and with arms built like logs. Averill Montgomery was similar in size and strength to Buck Jones, but there the resemblance ended, for Montgomery acted as mild as a kitten and was as soft-spoken as a whisper.

Joe raised his voice to be heard, "Welcome all to Sweetwater Station. Betty, it's good to see you again. Tisdale, I received your letter and will speak with you later." He looked around and saw Hannah on the steps. "Please, come into the house for refreshments, everyone."

Seeing Ivan and Hank hovering in the background near the bunkhouse, Rance told Joe he'd wait until later. He and Thad took their satchels from the front boot and marched toward their fellow drivers and guards to catch up on the news of the robbery and the stage line. They greeted Slim and decided to bunk in the same room to leave more space for Rusty and Grover, or Jim and Fizzure. Slim showed them the way and stopped to introduce them to Paul Ward, who had awakened from his nap at the sound of the coach arriving. They all drifted into the large room and visited until dinner was served.

Montgomery went to the forge and scrutinized Slim's work. The veterinarian was not a trained farrier, but he was skilled through experience. He wandered in the door of the bunkhouse and hearing the sounds from the large room, he joined the other men. The short, dumpy man eventually found his way to the room and after introductions, was assigned a room. If Rusty and Grover spent the night, the rooms would be full.

In the house, Hannah, Ruth and Betty were renewing their acquaintance while the children ate biscuits and drank water. The men had coffee and the ladies tea. After a pleasant hour, Hannah and Ruth began the final preparation for the noon meal, while Betty watched her children and Fuller, a needlework project in her hands.

The men went into the inner garden, since it was the only place they were assured of privacy. The initial discussion was much as Joe had imagined. Tisdale wanted to see the site of the tragedy and the wreckage before his final decision would be made. It turned out the short, dumpy man was owner and operator of a carpentry and machinery factory. His name was Fagan McGee. He would determine if the coach could be restored enough to be driven or pulled by mules to his shop. If not, a temporary shop might be built at Sweetwater. As a last resort, it would be torn apart and the material used in its construction hauled to his shop.

Shortly after the discussion, the sound of Rusty Backgammon's trumpet was heard and to his surprise, the yard at Sweetwater was filled with wagons, a red stage coach, and several horses.

The general public had descended on the station in earnest. The initial article that had appeared in the Denver newspaper had been telegraphed to other major outlets, and curiosity seekers and newsmen wanted the site examined and photographed.

Hannah and Ruth found themselves in a constant state of cookery. Betty helped by watching the children and making sandwiches of sliced beef and ham and cheese. A jar of pickles was brought from the root cellar, and one oven of the stove was used to make a selection of pies and cakes, while the other made biscuits and cornbread. The fireplace was used for pots of soup and venison stew which took longer to simmer and cook.

There were seven people on the stage from Mozier: six men and one woman. Betty and her husband were given the last room in the house; the men, after a conversation with Wallace Tisdale were taken directly to Buckboard Station with Ivan driving and Hank acting as shotgun messenger. Joe and Slim changed the mules and after a meal, Rusty and Grover returned to Mozier, empty. Near sunset Jim Owens and Fizzure Rodriguez arrived, carrying six men and, thankfully, no women. The rooms in the bunkhouse were filled, and several men were asleep on the floor in the large room. Rusty made a second trip that week with four men and two women, and had three men passengers on the return east to Mozier.

The trip to the wreckage was now imperative if any information could be found before the mob descended. Joe, Tisdale, Montgomery, McGee, Potter and Ray, and Paul Ward as the only living witness, set out early the next morning, following the now-obliterated trail. Joe led them straight to the site by memory. A line of men on horseback followed more cautiously behind. Already, the tracks of the lawmen had obscured any sign the bandits had made, but the wreckage of the coach and the mounds containing the victims were examined and photographed. Speculation was rampant.

Rumors abounded. Paul found himself the center of attention; and his photograph appeared throughout the nation, as the sole survivor.

Montgomery and McGee surveyed the wreckage and determined the coach could be repaired. Strong heavy chains and ropes were utilized and with the help of two mules, the coach was pulled upright and stood once more on its wheels. Montgomery went over the wheels and axles and determined it could be driven, with care. The parade of stage officials and curiosity seekers made their way slowly back to Sweetwater. The men were given rooms in the bunkhouse. While Montgomery and McGee set up a temporary shop near the forge, the red coach carrying Tisdale, Betty and their children returned to Denver via the forest road. Within days, the news-men and photographers disappeared, and the station returned to some semblance of order.

Hawk Blandon requested an audience with Joe after the evening meal. "Joe, I think your men can handle the animals and chores, now. I'll be leaving on the next stage. Tisdale has offered me a position in Denver, and I've decided to take it. I've enjoyed working on the Sweetwater; it's a good station, in spite of all the recent upheaval. I'll never forget the experience." He held out his hand, and Joe accepted his resignation.

"Blandon, I couldn't have managed without the help. Thank you. I wish you well in your new position with the company." The next morning he was chopping wood and hauling water from the spring to help Ivan and Hank wash the black coach.

On the Thursday came the familiar sound of Rusty's trumpet, and the residents gathered in the yard to welcome the new guests: two women and a girl, and the child's father. Katie Wynn was tall but plain, wearing dark clothing that did nothing to accent her pale skin and vibrant freckles. Wynona Freidmont was near blind, with thick spectacles. She had hired Katie to be her companion on the trip to Denver. Both seemed content to converse between themselves, and they didn't engage anyone else in conversation. Norman Fitzwilliam was a merchant looking for a house for himself and his daughter, and a large building to set up a small shop for the business of optometry. Montgomery gave him an address of a small place that he thought was still vacant, and McGee told him of a modest house near his own.

Rusty and Grover spent the night, and once again the rooms in the bunkhouse and the house were filled to overflowing. Hannah cooked a roast beef, with her usual pot of beans and soup, turnips, squash, and fresh tomatoes and onions from the garden. Grover toured the wheelwright's temporary shop and forge. Ivan, Hank and Joe filled Rusty in on the events of the last week while he puffed away on his cigar. He told them that Youngblood had received word from Tisdale that the north-south route of Paul Ward from Pueblo to Mozier would be permanently re-routed through the Sweetwater Station; and the Mozier station would be used only on the east-west run. The northern route to Cheyenne would be canceled altogether, since the railroad was complete from Cheyenne to Denver.

Paul accepted the news as calmly as he could. Tisdale had promised him a position when he was well enough to drive, and that time was coming soon. He exercised his arm daily, and several times had driven the black coach for a few miles, with Ivan ready to take the reins if he grew tired. All the men of the stage line could sense the changes, but weren't overly concerned. As long as there were local lines between villages and towns, they would have jobs. The western territories and

Texas were open and still had long distance stage routes. Rusty bragged that he would retire to Denver and live in luxury the rest of his days, but Joe could see the fear and sorrow in his eyes.

That evening, Jim Owens and Fizzure Rodriguez arrived with four men who had heard about the robbery and were disappointed that the coach was in the process of being repaired. They examined it closely and heard the story from the source, Paul Ward, and went on their way east the next morning with Rusty and Grover. The sound of the trumpet died away on the high mountain air, and the call of the birds in the trees could be heard to replace it.

Ivan and Hank prepared to head west with the two women and the merchant Fitzwilliam and his daughter. McGee gave a final glance around the station grounds and squeezed himself into the space beside the opposite window. Blandon threw his carpetbag into the rear boot with the other luggage, and turned to shake hands with Joe and his family. Paul Ward left to take up his new position when Tisdale reassigned him. He'd live in a hotel until then. He waved to them from the window. There were tears in Ruth's eyes as she bid him farewell. The coach disappeared among the pines and spruce of the forest, and the residents settled down once again to their routine.

It was an anticlimax, and a sober group sat at the supper table that night, only Joe and Hannah, his parents and son, with Slim and the coachmen after all the excitement of the last weeks since the robbery. Missing was Standing Tree and his dignified orations. Peter sat under the tree and smoked his cigar, silent and alone. He would take the first watch of the night. Slim and the coachmen spent some time in the large room before going to their separate rooms; the bunkhouse seemed to echo in its emptiness, and the wind whispered in the treetops. Joe took one last sashay around the perimeter of the station, the dog trotting beside him. He said good-night to his father and left the light of a single lantern for him. He and Hannah cuddled in the bed and heard Peter come in. All was quiet, and the stars brightly shone in a clear sky accompanied by a silent sliver of a moon beaming over the land.

Fourteen

Toward morning, thunder was heard in the distance, and rain began to pound on the roof. Joe rose to take the early morning watch; he drank a glass of water and picked out some biscuits from the basket on the table. He went to the larder and sliced a couple of thin slices of cooked cold ham and a small chunk of cheese. He put on his coat and hat, took his rifle from the shelf and went out into a pouring rain. He called to Hank, who had replaced Peter on guard, and received a faint reply. Hank was hovering under the eaves of the barn for the small shelter it provided. Joe joined him and gave him some of his stash of food, and sent him off to bed. The rain soon tapered off, and Joe was able to come into the open. The moon appeared from behind the clouds, and the stars soon followed. It was going to be a good day.

Light appeared in a red-streaked sky in the east, and Joe walked along the corral fence, singing softly to calm the animals. As the sky brightened, he could make out objects more clearly: the barn, the bunkhouse, the large station house and the stands of trees. Smoke began to curl from the stovepipe, and he heard the door open and knew Hannah was awake. His heart quickened, and he moved to see her, Fuller's small hand in hers, as she made her way to the outhouse. A lump came into his throat, and pride swelled his chest. He saw her emerge and return to the house. His eyes scanned the horizon, and soon the light was extended over the land, leaving the only darkness in the forest behind him. He saw his father come out with a milk bucket in his hand, and he waited to enter the house with him.

"Good morning, Papa. Did you sleep well?"

"Sure did, son. After all that noise and excitement, it was good to relax with the family again. Did I hear rain? The ground is damp." Joe joined him as they walked to the house.

"Sure did. A slow rain, good for the garden. It'll be muddy for a few hours. Poor Hank was out in it when I came out." He held the door for Peter and entered behind him. He hung his hat on the peg and draped his coat over a chair to dry completely. He called to Hannah, "Look what I found wandering outside, darling. Coffee hot?"

"Come, dear, and sit down. You must be cold. Thanks, Papa, for the milk." She brought the coffee pot and poured them some of the brew. "Mama's still asleep, I think."

"Let her rest. She was worn out from the visitors. I'll have two eggs this morning, daughter. I smell biscuits. Are they almost ready?" Peter took a sip of his coffee and cursed. He looked up guiltily. "It's hot."

Joe laughed. He blew on his own cup and took a cautious sip. He heard a sound at the door and turned. It was a more rested-looking Slim. He slipped into his seat at the table and waited for the coffee to be poured. "Had rain during the night," he commented, but since it was a statement they all agreed with, he received no answer.

157

Hannah put the pot of porridge on the table, and everyone took a turn dipping a portion into their bowls. She finished cooking the bacon and brought the platter to the table. It was pounced on as though they were small children. Fuller started banging on his empty bowl with his spoon. Joe reached for it and dipped some porridge in and poured some milk on top. "Eat hearty, son, someday you'll have teeth enough to eat the Big Boy food." Fuller grinned his almost toothless grin. Ruth sheepishly appeared, muttered an apology for being late; her hair was in place, and she was wearing a clean blue calico dress. She went to the peg and pulled on her apron. Hannah tied it for her and finished frying the men's eggs.

"Mama, you look rested. Did you hear the rain in the night?"

"No, did it rain? I slept soundly. Where are the boys?" She called the other men who worked at the station "boys." As though she had called them from the bunkhouse, they began to appear, first Hank and then Ivan. They dug into the porridge pot and followed up with hot biscuits and bacon. Montgomery wandered in, looking sleepy and with his clothes rumpled. He had worked on the coach until late the night before. The conversation drifted from the rain to the chores to be done, to speculation about what Tisdale would do, and there it stopped. The men finished and went out to their separate destinations. Montgomery returned to his work shop. Joe chopped some more wood; Peter sat under the cottonwood for a smoke; Ivan went to the black coach to see if the rain had splattered mud on its surface; Hank went to the bunkhouse and read a book in the large room; Slim went to the corrals. The dog wandered around from tree to tree, sniffing the ground.

The women sat down to eat, and Hannah fed Fuller some

small crumbs of bacon. His fat fingers took them into his mouth, and he chattered away in his own style. They rose to clear the table and wash the dishes. While Ruth washed, Hannah dried and tended to Fuller, who now had porridge on his chin and ear.

Rusty was late that week and complained of the wind that blew the dust hard against his coach. "Dagnabbit," he grumbled as he dropped from the box. "If it ain't the mud, it's the sand. So a feller cain't see the prairie chickens in the bushes."

Joe gave him a friendly hand with the luggage from the rear boot. Grover carried the mail bag into the house without a word.

Three men were on the stage, one dressed in a black suit and white shirt named Henry Lane, and the others in the common trousers and flannel shirts of miners or farmers were called Pridmore and Sorrell. During supper Grover told them of a letter he got from a buddy he'd known in the war. It was all about the two railroads, the Union Pacific and the Central Pacific meeting in Utah at a place called Promontory Point, and the inauguration of the new president, Ulysses S. Grant. Those men who had fought for the North celebrated, but those like Joe who had fought for the South were not so pleased. The mail sack was opened, and the newspapers were full of the news. The men staying in the bunkhouse read the stories over and over and began to argue.

After supper, while Joe was sitting in the house talking to Rusty, a fight broke out in the bunkhouse, and Hank came running for Joe. He went in the door and down the long hallway to the large room and found it a shambles. The tables were overturned, and the books and newspapers were scattered on the floor. Lane in the black suit, his collar spotted with blood, and Sorrell the farmer were going at it, blow by blow. Joe and

Grover separated them, and Joe said to take their differences outside. No sooner did the men get out the door until the fight began again. Joe let them finish. The black suit lost and sat brooding in the large room. Slim tended to the cuts and scrapes on his face and knuckles, while the other man went to his room and locked the door. The other passenger only watched and later pulled out a deck of cards and started a game.

As the sun was becoming brighter in the eastern sky, Joe hitched the horses to the coach and Ivan drove it out of the shed. He ran over it for flaws and greased the axles. Hank came out of the bunkhouse with his satchel in his hand, ate his breakfast, picked up the mail bag from the house and stored them in the front boot. He had his shotgun hoisted across his shoulder and looked fierce and determined. It wasn't often they had a disturbance at the station, but his job was to guard the mail, and he stood like a sentinel until Ivan finished eating. The man in the black suit came out of his room, clean and neat, with a piece of Slim's sticking tape on a cut on his chin. He looked chastened and sober. The other fighter came out with his carpetbag in his hand. As he crossed in front of the black coach, he dropped the bag near the coach and quickened his steps to the house.

Pridmore entered the Public Room and quietly ate his breakfast and waited by the house for the order to board the stage. Slim and Joe observed it all while they started their ritual of checking the coach, inspecting the horses and loading the luggage into the rear boot. Montgomery came out of the house with a small satchel and a large carpetbag in his hands. He had declared the brown coach ready for service again. It seemed to Joe to be the proper ending to the saga of the robbery and killing of Manning. They stood talking for a moment after all the luggage was secure in the rear boot.

"What should we do about the shop? Do you think Tisdale will send a driver for the coach?" Joe looked at the vehicle parked under the shed that Montgomery had used as his forge and workplace. It had no walls, just a roof and four pillars to hold it up. The coach had been freshly painted brown. The interior was mostly the same as it had been with a few stitches on the seats, where they had been torn by the upset.

"I'd leave it, Joe. The shop, that is. I don't know his plans for the coach. He'll probably send someone to drive it away." He sighed. "I hate to go back to the city; I've enjoyed your wife's cooking. Good luck to you." He held out his hand, and Joe shook it with a sparkle in his eyes.

"Take your wife to the opera house soon; she'll like it. It's not my favorite kind of music, but the women are pretty." He stepped back, and the wheelwright stepped into the coach. Ivan climbed into the box, and Hank swung up beside him; and with a whirl of dust, they were off on the forest road.

It was Rusty's time to go, and he stood with his cigar in his mouth, watching the black coach disappear. There were no passengers for the return trip to Mozier. He and Grover would be alone.

"That was a humdinger of a fight last night, old son. You think those fellows'll be able to ride all the way to Denver closed up in that coach?" He puffed on his cigar and blew the smoke into the air above his head.

"I don't know, Rusty. But, when they discover the saloon at Weaver's place, there might be more fighting. I'm of mixed emotions myself. First, the railroad spells doom for our business, and now with a Yankee Army general as president, there's bound to be more fighting. A fist fight's sometimes a good thing; clears the air, but if drinking and guns get involved, that brings real trouble. Well, keep your eyes open on the road. Grover, you watch sharp for snakes and other critters."

Grover gave him a wave and swung into the high seat. Rusty made one more check of the lead mule and climbed into the box. He picked up his bugle and played a merry tune as he drove away. Joe turned aside and watched Slim walk to the barn. He followed him. "Say, I think I'd like a ride after all that excitement. Care to join me? The work will wait a while."

Slim nodded in the affirmative, and they saddled Mack and the sorrel stallion named Juno. They led the horses out of the barn, and waved at Peter squatting under the cottonwood tree as they galloped away.

Peter went into the bunkhouse and began to clean the rooms and change the bed clothes of the guests. The workers took care of their own rooms. He righted the furniture, put the books back on the shelf and cleaned up the glass from a broken lamp, shaking his head at the young men's foolishness. He tied the sheets in a large bundle and took it to the house for the wash. He returned with the broom and swept the floor of the large room. The newspapers that had caused all the fighting, he tore into strips and burned in the fireplace. Finally, he went to the supply shed and brought out a lantern for the room and set it on the table. He looked around the room and left the building.

Joe and Slim returned from their ride, brushed their respective mounts and put them in their stalls. With a mutual agreement they went through the herd and brought out two horses to be shod. While Slim started a fire in the forge, Joe thought about what Montgomery had said about the shop. He walked around it and ideas started popping in his head. He went to the house and spoke to his father. Within two days, the once temporary repair shop was empty of the forge which was moved to one of the horse sheds and set up for Slim's use. A floor and one wall were built to make a snug cabin for his parents. By the time for the stage to come from Mozier again, two walls were finished. It rained all day on the Monday, so work was delayed. On Tuesday they started again but stopped for the other chores necessary for the return of the coaches.

Fifteen

Hannah and Ruth were in the kitchen cleaning up after breakfast and keeping an eye on Fuller playing on the floor with the metal soldiers of Napoleon's army, lining them up in rows, red shirts against blue shirts. Suddenly, they heard the sound of horses' hooves, and Ruth ran to the door and opened it. It was the marshal's posse, and Standing Tree was slowly dismounting.

"It's the law back, and Standing Tree." Ruth's voice was filled with excitement. "I've missed the Indian more than I care to admit."

Hannah picked up her son, and they went onto the porch to watch the men gather in the yard.

Joe heard the men returning from their investigation, took one last blow at the log under his ax, threw the wood into the pile and sank the ax into the wood to be sharpened later. He looked up and saw Standing Tree, and he was glad. He grinned and stood watching as the men dismounted. He saw Hannah and Ruth out of the corner of his eye come out of the house. Ivan came running and stopped in his tracks. Joe noticed and was pleased to see his rifle in his hand. His own was not two feet from the ax. He picked it up and held it in the crook of his arm, barrel down. He started walking toward the men, who were in the process of dismounting or walking around to stretch their muscles. A couple of the men swung their arms out to loosen them.

"Hello, Captain Sizemore. Did you have a successful trip?" Joe could see the fatigue in the man's eyes, and possibly a disappointment, also.

"No. We rode for miles, but didn't catch up with them. They went to Rockland Station all right, stole three of the horses; just missed Tisdale and his party. Moore said they'd been there. Looks like the bandits have moved west out of the Territory, over the mountain pass. Either that, or they're headed south into New Mexico. Either way, the trail grew cold among the boulders and thick forest. We came back through here to escort your tracker home. He's a good man, 'spite of his age. Glad he went with us. My men will set up camp tonight, and we'll head out tomorrow for Denver. If you have a place for me, I'd sure like a bath and some hot food."

Joe noticed that Hannah and Ruth had returned to the house, and he knew she'd have hot coffee soon. "I don't know about the food, but I'm sure my wife put the coffee pot on the stove when she saw you. Let me speak to the Indian, and I'll be with you." He saw that Hank had gone to welcome Standing Tree, and he continued on to the lawmen. Ivan was talking with the deputy, Browning. Slim took Standing Tree's horse to the water trough and gave him some grain. He began to brush him down.

Joe looked at Standing Tree and gazed into his black eyes. He looked tired but healthy. He reached out his hand in welcome. The Indian took it and pumped it up and down

165

vigorously.

"Welcome back, my friend. Are you hungry?"

"Standing Tree hungry. Belly hurt. No find evil man. Go many miles. Horse need rest. Good to see white man's house."

Joe smiled, and the Indian started walking toward the house in his slow, shuffling way. Joe followed. He took the medicine bag from around his neck and handed it to his friend, who took it with a grunt and hung it around his neck.

Joe held the door for him. Out of the corner of his eye, he saw Captain Sizemore leave his men and follow them. Inside, Hannah was cooking slices of ham and onions. She put in some flour, stirred it up and poured in milk to make gravy. Ruth cut slices of bread and put them on a platter. Fuller was playing with a couple of smooth blocks of wood. Jack sat on his tail by the fireplace. When he saw Standing Tree, he started a ruckus, barking and chasing his tail, until Ruth picked him up and took him to the inner garden.

Standing Tree laid his bow and quiver of arrows on the shelf and took his regular seat as though he hadn't been gone several weeks. Joe's eyes filled with the sight of him, his heart beating fast. He welcomed the captain and told him to take a seat. Peter came into the room and sat down. He took out a cigar and handed it to the Indian. Joe saw the surprise on Sizemore's face, but he knew the significance of the gesture, and Standing Tree did, too. His black eyes shone with pleasure. The old Indian watched Hannah work, and she turned with a smile and poured him a glass of water, which he downed without stopping. He set the glass on the table and burped.

Joe saw Sizemore look sharply at him and jump when Standing Tree pronounced in his deep voice, "Water is good. Boy grow fat. You good cook, Scarred Woman. Big Mother,

166

how you do? Long time Standing Tree not see white friends at spring. I happy to see Big Father from across mighty river. You teach Yo Hadley smoke while I gone?" He burst out laughing, and the family joined him. Sizemore gaped and began to laugh, too.

"No. Joe doesn't smoke, but I'll join you after you eat. Sizemore, do you smoke? It's a joke between us. My son never acquired the habit, and Standing Tree sees it as a fault in my character that I didn't teach him." He grinned at Ruth as she set the platter of bread in front of him, and turned for the tin of molasses. The family had eaten breakfast, but the two travelers dug in with gusto, while the conversation centered on Tisdale's visit. The next morning, Captain Sizemore and his men left the station for Denver.

Two days later, the residents were surprised to see several supply wagons roll into the yard, with some outriders on horses. A tall, thin man stepped down and walked to the corral where Joe was currying his horse, Mack. He and Slim had taken an early morning ride. Slim was standing by Modred, the yearling.

Joe went to meet the stranger. "Hello. I'm Joe Hadley. Can I help you?" He glanced at the other men, waiting for their leader to give them instructions.

"Is this the station called Sweetwater?" He took a piece of paper from his pocket and looked at it. "I've never been this far north. I've come from Pueblo in the south. My boss, Hicks, said I was to bring you these supplies and give you instructions on the new stage route. The new coach driver's name is Torrance, but we call him Tex. Comes from around the Fort Worth area. He's taking Paul Ward's place. I understand you know Paul. Hicks told us about the trouble he had. Sure hate Manning got himself killed. He was a good man. What do you want me to do with the supplies?" He looked around as though he thought Joe wanted them scattered on the grounds.

"Did I hear you say another driver is coming? Does that mean I'm supposed to house the coach and Torrance here permanently?'

"Yeh, that's what I said, didn't I? Tisdale and Hicks decided that the stage will skip Mozier Station and come directly here. They closed down the northern end of the route, so you're to keep Tex and the coach." He gazed at his audience which had grown to include Ivan, Hank and Slim.

"But, what about Charles Youngblood at Mozier Station? And, Rusty and Grover? They'll still come to this station, won't they?

"Don't know. The boss just said I was to deliver the supplies to Sweetwater and go on back to Pueblo."

Joe pointed to the supply shack he and Jeremiah Fuller had built in the first year he'd managed the station. "Put the tinned goods and bags of produce in the shed; I'll ask my wife what she needs in the house. You got any grain, hay, tools, things that should go in the barn? It's over there; the big brick building. Anything else, leave by the house and we'll sort it out later." He left the man standing and walked to the first wagon.

"Hello, men. I'm Joe Hadley. What have you got in the wagons?"

A large, slender man dressed in casual working clothes dropped from the wagon seat. "This is Sweetwater, then?" Joe nodded. "You're Hadley?"

"Yes." Joe was puzzled. He had said he was Hadley.

The man grinned and stuck out his hand. "I'm glad to know you. Old Scrappy told us about you. He said you wus the best damn stage manager he ever knew. Always fair, even-handed and friendly; never interfere with the drivers and the guards. I'm Bernard; Tom Bernard. I'm a cobbler by trade, but I couldn't resist taking the chance of meeting Joe Hadley, could I?"

"Scrappy? Do you mean Phineas Knell, the man who carries that rabbit-skin bag while he's on the coach? Where is he? Is he on this route from Pueblo?"

"No. He broke his arm falling off the coach when it hit a big hole in the road. The doctor didn't set it right; it's all crooked, so he settled down in Pueblo with a desk job; sells tickets and makes out schedules and things. Works for Hicks. Got him a wife named Martha."

"I'm sorry to hear he took a fall. I didn't know him for long; he was transferred somewhere, and we lost track of him. My wife will be pleased to know he's settled down."

While they were talking, Slim unlocked the door to the shed, and a couple of men started to shift things to make room for the new supplies. Several other men carried the boxes and barrels and crates to the shack. The last wagon was backed near the barn, and two strong men started hauling bags of grain and bales of hay to the building. One of the bags fell from the wagon and split open. Joe heard a long string of curses from the driver of the wagon.

"Damn." Joe frowned as he shook his head. "Was hoping to have that feed for the horses."

Hank ran to the barn for a couple of shovels, and he and Ivan helped the men scoop up the grain and put it in a new bag. The residue they took to the animals. Slim stood talking to the leader. Joe hadn't caught his name. Once the wagons were empty and turned to go back south, he invited Bernard and the leader into the house.

169

"Hannah, this is Tom Bernard. He's a cobbler and knows Scrappy. Knell got married and works in Pueblo. You remember the guard on our coach from Mozier the first time?" He picked up the barking dog and patted his head.

Hannah had Fuller on her hip while she set out cups on the table for coffee. She looked from Joe to Bernard, and then to the other man. "Scrappy? Of course, I remember. He's in Pueblo?"

"Bernard says he broke his arm and it didn't heal right, so he works in the stage office." He turned to the leader. "I didn't catch your name, sir. This is my wife, Hannah and my son, Fuller. Dog's name is Jack. The other lovely lady is my mother, Ruth Hadley."

The man gave him a quizzical look and said, "Name's Percy. Percy Fielding." He seemed to be overly interested in Hannah's scared face, but Joe kept his temper.

"Have a seat." Standing Tree rose from his place by the fireplace and sat down at the table. Joe heard a growl from Fielding. He turned and gave him a fierce glance. Hannah put Fuller in his tall chair and gave him the wooden blocks. Ruth poured coffee into the cups and returned to the stove, a frown on her face. Bernard seemed to sense the tension in the air and started to talk of Pueblo and the facilities. Fielding seemed to relax with the discussion and soon rose to leave.

"Thanks for the coffee, ma'am. We best be on our way; it's a long way back. Hadley, Torrance should be here in the afternoon. I trust you'll have a place for him by then." He pulled his gloves from a pocket and drew them onto his hands. Joe had noticed the softness of his palms but hadn't taken in the significance until now. He walked them out.

The other men were squatted on the ground talking to Ivan,

Hank and Slim. They all rose when they saw Fielding come from the house. They scrambled to the wagons or the horses and mounted. Within minutes they were on their way south. Joe and his workers watched them go. He heard the door slam and saw Standing Tree come down the steps and go to his tree and light his pipe. The dog lay beside him and went to sleep.

"Well, fellows, looks like we got ourselves a stage coach and driver, and probably another guard, too. Fielding didn't mention him. What do you think, Ivan?" He looked around the yard, took off his hat and ran his fingers through his hair.

"He gave me a map of the route and a list of things we're supposed to do here. I thought it odd that he didn't give them to you. One of the hands said he's new to the business, came from Virginia or somewhere east. I suspect he's frightened of you." Slim laughed, and then Ivan laughed, too. Hank looked puzzled.

"Me? Fielding was frightened of me? Why?"

"From what we heard Bernard say and what the hands told us, that friend of yours, Scrappy, has built you up to be some kind of god of the stage business." Slim circled the dirt with the toe of his boot and grinned.

"What? That's nonsense." He looked at the men and grinned. "Damn. That's bad. Really? You think Fielding was frightened of me?" He laughed until his side ached, and he pressed one hand into it. His face felt warm, and he knew he was blushing. He walked to the corral and picked up a mare's hoof to check for stones in the shoe.

After supper, Slim handed Joe the map and schedule, and he discussed them with the men in the large room of the bunkhouse. "It appears, Ivan, you and Hank'll have to make the trip to Rockland twice a week. Once to take the people from Pueblo and the south, and once to ferry the people from the east

171

and the Mozier station, else the first group would have to stay two days and nights, and we don't have the room. If it was only men, they could be put up in the bunkhouse, but the ladies need more comfort. Lordy, I don't know what we'll do if more females start to traveling. That'll mean, Slim, that we need two teams of horses, fit and able to make the trip each week. You go through the inventory of horses able to pull the coach, and I'll do the same, and we'll compare notes. The mule situation will remain the same, unless the west to east traffic picks up. That means my father will have to take on more chores around the house and gardens, and we'll have twice the responsibility of the animals and coaches. Think about it, friends. We'll see what happens when the new men arrive."

About midday, several riders showed up on horseback. A bow-legged cowboy leaped from the saddle, dressed in denims, a large brimmed hat and worn, scratched boots. A slender man of uncertain age dismounted and took a shotgun from the leather holster on the saddle. He was more conventionally dressed in corduroy trousers and blue plaid shirt, a leather vest on his chest and black boots, worn and dusty. Joe didn't have time to distinguish the other riders as they dismounted and began to move around the area. A couple walked to the spring; one stooped beside the stream and scooped up some water to drink. Joe's attention was caught by a scrawny, middle-aged man who walked toward him.

"You Hadley?" The man looked Joe over closely.

"Yes, I am." Joe noticed the man examine the buildings and the half-finished cabin before turning his eyes back to him.

"Hello, I'm Hicks. I've heard a lot about you from Phineas Knell, my clerk. He says you run this station like it was your own. He says you treat the men fair and square and feed them well. I came to see for myself if it's true." He squinted toward Slim and the coachmen who were emerging from the bunkhouse one by one.

Joe didn't know what to say. If he agreed, it would seem as though he were vain; if he contradicted him, he'd be untruthful. He stood still. Suddenly, the man turned his head toward the forest. Joe caught sight of Standing Tree coming from the forest where he'd been since early morning, a wild turkey over his shoulder. His friend was stumbling along as though his legs could barely move.

"Pardon me." Joe took off at a run, followed by Slim. Ivan and Hank stayed where they were. Joe relieved Standing Tree of his burden and handed the bird to Slim, who headed toward the fire pit, where he threw the carcass on the ground. Joe put his arm around the old man's shoulder and helped him to his tree.

"Sit down." He brushed aside the blanket and felt of the pulse in his neck. It was fast and heavy. He pulled the neckerchief from his pocket and yelled at Ivan. "Ivan, get me another blanket and some cloths. Hank, get a bucket of cool water." By that time, Slim had run for the barn and his medicine bag. Joe only noticed from the corner of his eye the approach of the man called Hicks. The other men gathered about.

"What's wrong? I saw him come from the forest. Is he sick? What can I do?" Ruth was breathless and pale. Peter was beside her, a frown on his face.

"I don't know, Mama. Tell Hannah to go ahead with dinner. We have a lot of visitors." He rose to his feet. "Mama, go into the house. There's nothing you can do here, and Hannah needs you." She hesitated and he kissed her on the cheek. "Papa, take Mama in the house. He brought home a turkey. It'll need plucking and cleaning before it spoils."

Peter nodded, and he and Ruth withdrew to the house. Peter returned to light a fire in the pit and heat water to soften the feathers for plucking. He kept his eyes on Joe and the rest as he worked. One of the men; the one who'd gotten a drink from the creek, went to help him. Joe was half aware of them talking as Slim returned with his bag.

Ivan came from the house with a wool blanket in one hand, and some clean cloths in another. Hank breathlessly rushed up with the bucket of water, and Joe began to bathe the Indian's hot face. Slim waited a moment and said, "Let me look at him, Joe."

Joe stepped back and looked around at the crowd of men surrounding him and frowned. Hicks stood out to him, and he thought it a good time to continue their earlier conversation.

"What were you saying, sir? You're Hicks from Pueblo? Come to the bunkhouse and we'll talk. Your men are welcome to set up camp near the spring, unsaddle their horses and sit a spell. Hank, show the men where to go. Ivan, you stay and help Slim. Come to me the minute I'm needed." He turned and started strolling toward the large building a few yards away. The men followed, Hicks in front, like a duck with her ducklings in tow.

Joe opened the bunkhouse door and walked the length of the hallway, his mind on Standing Tree. He didn't like the way the man was breathing, but he knew Slim was the only doctor they had. If anything could be done, he was the one to do it. He went to the fireplace, where the men had a large pot of coffee simmering. He grabbed a cloth from the mantle, removed the pot from the coals and set it on a metal plate on the table. He looked around and saw several cups on a shelf. He was surprised to see one of the men, the one in denims and worn boots, brush him aside and start setting the cups on the table. He had taken off his hat and thrown it on the sofa. One by one, the men came in and took a seat at the tables, and one man lifted the hat from the sofa, carried it to the pegs on the wall and placed it there and sat down.

Joe looked at Hicks. The man had an odd look on his face.

Hicks looked at his men and a smile crossed his face. "Well, that answers my first question. Don't know who that Injun is, but you obviously care for him. Phineas didn't mention him. Who is he?" He sat at the table and took one of the cups and blew on it.

Joe glanced around and sat down. "He's called Standing Tree, of the Arapahoe tribe. He's my friend." He didn't feel he needed to say anything else. Apparently, neither did Hicks, for he started introducing his crew.

"This is Torrance, your new driver taking Paul Ward's place. We call him Tex. Next to him, that lanky fellow is Calvin Meldrick. We call him Mel. He's the new guard, just hired to take Manning's place. He hails from Louisiana." He continued to name the rest, but Joe couldn't remember all the names. There were six in all, counting Hicks. He stood and shook hands with each as their name was called and sat back down. He took a sip of coffee.

"I'm the Southern Regional Agent, out of Pueblo, but we dip down into New Mexico to Taos, and east to Fort Dodge in Kansas. The stages are erratic; only a few stations. The men have to drive long distances; hot and dusty for some; high mountain passes for others. Tisdale wrote me about the hold-up and Manning. He was a good man. I'd known him for years, from when he first showed up after the war, looking for a job. I haven't known Ward as long. He's in Denver now. Tisdale is trying to decide where to put him. 'Twouldn't be right to put him on the same run where the killing happened. He'd shy away from the area. At least, that's my thinking. Tisdale said he'd send you instructions as soon as he came up with a plan. Me, I'm too impatient to wait. I need to get that route to running regular again. I see you have the coach here. Is it ready to roll?"

Joe was bewildered. The man was shooting too many facts at him at once, when his mind was on his Indian friend. He looked around. All the men had their eyes on him. He pulled himself together and began to speak.

"Yes. Montgomery left a few days ago. He's the wheelwright that repaired it. He said it was ready."

"Good. Good. We'll start off tomorrow, then. Tex'll drive with Mel as shotgun messenger. I'll ride inside and a couple of the others." He named two men, Davis and Purl, and they nodded. "The rest'll act as outriders. It'll be a new route so we need strong, experienced horses, the best you have. The first one or two trips will be new to them, so choose wisely. Now, the men'll set up camp, and Larry'll wash these cups and the pot so's your men don't have to do it. I thank you for the hot drink. We wus thirsty." The men all mumbled their gratitude, and everyone rose to leave. The men scattered toward the spring and their horses, except one, whom Joe assumed was Larry.

As they left the building, Joe saw that Standing Tree was on his feet, and the men had disappeared. Peter was still beside the fire pit, working on the turkey. He saw Slim leaning against one of the corrals.

"Come with me, Hicks. I need to talk with my animal handler." Joe started that direction, and as he began to move, Slim came to meet them. "How is Standing Tree?" He relaxed

176

when Slim laughed.

"He's fine. Had the wind knocked out of him. He must have walked a long way. He's an old man, Joe, but he won't admit defeat. I don't guess we'll get him to stop going off alone when he chooses." He waited to be introduced.

"Hicks, this is my animal handler, Slim Grimshaw. He's a professional veterinarian; been here three years. He's the human doctor, too, when we need one. Best there is around these parts." He chuckled.

Slim gave him a grimace and shook hands with the stage official. "He only says that 'cause I'm the only one around these part. How do you do, sir?"

"Well, very well, 'specially after meeting your boss, here." Hicks grinned, and he pointed with his thumb to Joe. He released Slim's hand, stepping back and waiting for further instructions.

"Come up to the house, sir, and meet my wife and parents. Dinner ought to be ready soon. Would Tex and Mel like to join us? Hannah always makes plenty."

"No. Not this time, maybe tonight for supper. They'll be wanting to say good-bye to their friends. I'll join you, though; I heard about your wife's apple pies. I sent up a couple of small barrels with the supplies."

Joe gave him an odd expression. He'd forgotten that Bernard had come from Hicks. They entered the house, and the dog set up a racket at the sight of the stranger. He stood stiffly and challenged him. Joe picked him up and patted his head. "Quiet, old man, he's a friend."

Slim put his hat on a peg, and Joe turned to place his on the peg where it was always kept when he was in the house. Hicks noticed their actions, and took off his jacket and put it on the remaining peg and his hat over it.

"Hannah, this is Mr. Hicks from Pueblo. He's the one who sent the supplies we received this morning. Hicks, my wife Hannah, and my mother Ruth." He glanced to see the man's reaction to Hannah's face, but he said nothing. He greeted her cordially and sat down at the table when Hannah indicated he should do so. Joe put the dog on the floor and went to the wash pan and cleaned his hands. Slim sat down and answered Ruth's questions about Standing Tree. Joe heard a sound, and the man was coming in the door. He sat in his regular place. Joe saw Hicks' eyes widen in surprise, but the expression on his face didn't change.

Ruth gave Standing Tree a glass of water and set a glass of milk before Joe's plate. She poured coffee for the others. Peter came in with the plucked turkey in his hand and took it to the root cellar. He stepped to the wash basin, scrubbed his hands and arms and tossed the water into the slop jar used for dirty water.

"Damn good turkey, son. Hardly any damage to the body." He made a positive sign to the Indian, and Standing Tree grunted and blinked his black eyes in return.

"Big Father praise good. Many moon past, Standing Tree first kill Bird That Don't Fly. You cook for Standing Tree, Scarred Woman?"

Hannah smiled. "Yes. I will. You kill; I cook." And the Indian started laughing. They all joined in; although Joe wasn't sure Hicks knew why they were laughing. For him, it was a release of tension. He knew his friend was alright if he could laugh.

Hannah set a pot of venison stew in front of them, with corn fritters and fresh onions. Ruth placed hot biscuits and a jar of marmalade at the other end. Joe stood and dipped the stew from the pot into the bowls, and the men started eating. Ruth refilled the coffee cups and sat down to eat. Ivan and Hank came in, sat down and filled their bowls. Ivan looked at Hicks and began to speak.

"Slim, I saw a mule with a cut on his leg. I walked him to the barn. I think it's the same one who knocked the fence down before. Stubborn mules; nothing but trouble. I wish we could use only horses." He muttered under his breath.

"I'll get to it right away. Thanks. Joe, we might have to get rid of him if he continues to act up. I don't mind doctoring him, but this is the third time. He seems to behave in harness, but causes trouble in the corral. The others are nervous around him."

"I'll look at him and think about it. I hate to put him down if that's his only problem. We could keep him separated from the herd and use him for the plow or logging when only one is needed. Sooner or later, he's bound to run off if he can." He looked at Hicks and swallowed a sip of milk.

"We keep horses and mules at this station, sir. Same at Mozier. There's deep sand between them, and coaches need heavier animals, sure-footed and strong. Horses are used for the other routes. I've gone on four roundups for the feral horses that roam the low areas north and west of here. We breed a few of them with the horses or donkeys. The rest we train for the coaches or wagons." He scooped up another spoonful of stew and chewed it thoroughly. "Been lucky so far. Tisdale decides what's to be done with them after we finish with them. I have some good saddle horses in the barn, if you'd like to see them later."

"That sounds fine. I like good horseflesh when I find it. Do you race the horses? They have some races on holidays at Pueblo. The men enjoy the competition."

"No. These are working animals. A couple of fellows have wanted to race, but I object. I suppose if Tisdale or you want some good saddle horses for the purpose, they could be provided. I have a couple of yearlings with good blood lines. My business is to provide the animals; what's to be done with them is your headache." He finished his stew, and Hannah brought a steaming hot apple pie from the oven. He looked at her and grinned. Her eyes were twinkling.

"Ah, Phineas told me about your apple pies, ma'am." Hicks sat watching as Hannah cut the pie into equal sections and placed them on plates. Ruth used a heavy cloth to take a second one from the oven.

"We have you to thank for the apples, sir. Without the regular supplies we couldn't have them," Hannah said modestly, and Joe grinned. He poured the last of his milk onto his pie and dug in. Ruth set the pitcher on the table, and Slim and Hicks poured some on their pie. Hannah fed Fuller, and he started banging on his bowl for more. The dog stood beside the table, drool running from his mouth and onto the floor. Standing Tree finished his pie and rose.

"Big Father smoke now? I wait." He left with his blanket held tightly around his shoulders, and after a few minutes, Peter followed him out the door.

Joe gave Hannah and his mother a peck on the cheek and left the room. He started work on the new cabin, ignoring the presence of the visitors. One of the men, Purl, picked up a hammer and without speaking, helped him with the work. Peter came and between the three carpenters, they finished one wall and started another one.

Just before the sun dropped behind the wall of trees, he called it quits and went to select the horses for the coach's departure in the early morning hours. Hicks came to see what he was doing, and when he'd finished, he showed the man Mack and Eva as well as the two yearlings he'd mentioned. Several of the men took the horses out for a ride and came back with them coated with sweat. Joe suspected that they'd raced, but the horses belonged to the stage line, all except Mack, and Hicks was his employer, so he said nothing.

There was roast turkey and gravy for supper. Beans, cabbage, and mustard greens, corn bread, fresh bread and a yellow cake for dessert. Hicks drew away from the table and went outside where the sun was setting. It threw a red shadow across the far distant mountains tops, and gray clouds hovered overhead. Joe knew it would rain during the night. He told Hicks to tell his men to go into the bunkhouse if the wind came up. He circled the corrals, and Slim shut the goats in the shed, and put the chickens in their coop. Tex and Ivan tied the wheels of the coach to a nearby tree with ropes for extra security. Ivan explained how the storms could come suddenly and ferociously during the night without warning.

Joe took the first watch after explaining to the other men why they did so every night. Hicks agreed that it was a good precaution, especially after the robbery of the coach. Joe ordered Standing Tree to sleep in the bunkhouse, and after gazing at the sky a few minutes, the Indian obeyed. When he was relieved shortly before midnight by Peter, there was a brisk breeze from the southwest, and the stars had disappeared behind the clouds. He went to bed, but his sleep was restless, and when the rain began to fall and the wind blew against the shutters, he woke Hannah and they closed them tight against the wind. He left her with the boy and went to check on his visitors.

From the porch steps he saw that Peter had already awakened them, and two were scrambling to take down the tents and fold them. The one who served as cook was hastily gathering up his equipment and supplies. The others were running pell-mell for the bunkhouse. Joe saw there was no reason for him to get wet. He'd warned them. He went back to bed, for he had gotten only a couple of hours sleep.

Hannah rose early as usual and took the boy out. Joe emerged and built a fire in the stove and fireplace. When the Public Room began to warm nicely, he took a turn outside and saw puddles of water everywhere but no damage to the buildings or tree limbs down. He went to the coach and walked around it. He was joined by Tex, who admitted he hadn't slept well, worried about the vehicle. Tex climbed on top and noticed a few hail strikes but no real damage. He gazed with envy at the big black coach inside its shelter. He climbed down, and he and Joe went to the holding pen for the horses. They seemed nervous, and Joe sang to them. Tex listened a minute and began to sing, too.

Slowly, one after another of the men left the bunkhouse, a few with sheepish grins on their faces. Joe went to check on Standing Tree and saw the cook had started their breakfast in the huge fireplace in the large room. Standing Tree was squatted beside the fire, his pipe in his mouth. Relieved, Joe went to the barn and checked the animals in there. Next, he went to the goat pen, released the animals, opened the chicken coop and spread some corn for the chickens; and they began to venture into the cool air. The two roosters spread their wings and welcomed the sun. Leaving the rest of the chores to the others, he returned to the house, where he was in time to greet his father on the way to the goat shed. He spent some time with Fuller, crawling on the floor with him pretending to be a horse, with his son riding his back. They fell in a heap, and he pretended to be dead. The boy pushed up his eyelid, and Joe laughed and cuddled the boy, and carried him to his chair and placed a cloth around his chest. Hannah gave him a spoon to keep him busy, and Joe sat down.

"Good morning, darling. It's going to be a good day. The rain has done no damage, and the coach and the others will soon be on their way. Standing Tree's smoking in the bunkhouse. He'll be here soon. I don't think his turkey hunt did any lasting harm, but he's growing weaker. Is Mama still asleep?"

"Yes. Papa didn't wake her when he rose. What will we do, if they shut down Mozier Station? Will Rusty and Grover be out of work?"

"I don't know, dear. I suppose Tisdale will offer positions elsewhere. Grover will be fine; but it'd be hard for Rusty to adjust to a different route. I'll offer him a place here, but he'd probably see it as charity and refuse. We'll have to wait and see how things happen."

Peter came in with the milk, and their conversation was interrupted. They started talking about the men's journey south, and Standing Tree, Ivan and Hank came in followed later by Slim. Hicks came in to give Joe some last minute instructions, and as soon as they ate they prepared for the trip south.

Joe took his usual tour of the coach, checked the axles, looked at the horses and explained to Hicks why he did so. "I trust the drivers and the messengers, but if something happens on the road, I want to sleep at night, knowing they left my station as prepared as possible."

The men brought out their luggage from the bunkhouse and stored it in the boots: the driver and guard in the front, the others in the back. The horsemen who would ride saddled their mounts and rode a few yards to get the animals calmed down.

Mel held his shotgun in his hand, and with the other hand as support climbed onto the high seat. His face was grim, and his eyes gazed straight ahead. Hicks shook hands once more, the other men boarded the stage and the door was shut. Tex turned to Joe.

"I want to thank you for your hospitality. I'll tell Scrappy hello for you. He'll be pleased to know the station's in good shape. If our luck holds, I'll see you in a week. 'Bye, Joe." He shook hands, and with a grimace, he climbed into the box, released the brake and drove away leaving muddy ruts in the road. A wheel hit a puddle, and the coach tilted but righted itself, and Joe watched as it crossed the creek, splashing water onto the sides of the vehicle and soon was out of sight. He sighed, and restless after all the activity, went for his hammer and nails, and worked steadily on the last wall of the cabin until his back ached and his hands and face were grimy from the mud.

The next day, he pulled the old brick molds from their storage place in the shed and lined them up along the opposite bank of the creek. He spent the major part of the afternoon turning soil and filling the molds, until about two dozen molds lay in the hot sun to dry. Hank crossed the creek and watched, then retreated to the bunkhouse. That night around the supper table Joe explained how he planned to make the brick fireplace for the small cabin. He told them of how he, Buck Jones, Rosie and Jeremiah Fuller had built the barn. Hank was seen looking closely at the walls, and the next morning, dressed in old denims and a red flannel shirt, he helped Joe dump the dried bricks from the molds and fill them once again. Peter worked diligently making a bed and a couple of chairs for his new home. Ivan spent his time reading or playing cards in the bunkhouse. Slim worked with the animals.

The peaceful scene of working men was interrupted on Thursday afternoon by the sound of Rusty's loud, discordant trumpet. Joe knew by the sound that Rusty was unhappy. When the door of the coach was opened, two men and three women stepped down. The men immediately went to the bunkhouse and didn't come out until supper was served. All of average height, the women were dressed in severe white blouses and dark skirts, with dark coats and small brimmed hats, as though they were in uniforms. Grover whispered to Joe that they were members of the Women's Suffrage Movement. One, who appeared to be the leader, was strident and critical of the station and the treatment of the animals. Her name was Dagmar, the others, Lucile and Gertrude. They were on their way to Denver for a rally to be held in the large Grange Hall, Grover said.

Rusty was on a rant. "Damn woman, screeching about women's rights, brandishing her cane as though she were Moses hisself, scared poor Irma Youngblood until she was in tears. You watch that woman, Joe, she's a tyrant. We're well rid of her. If I wus a drinking man, I'd sink into the doldrums, for sure. Says liquor is the Devil's work. Mebbe. Mebbe, but if the Good Lord hadn't planned for men to drink, why did he bless the wine at the banquet? I'm going back to Mozier; ain't staying the night with that woman around." The two men quickly ate a meal, and as soon as the mules were hitched, Rusty and Grover headed east to Mozier Station, with Grover driving.

It was apparent to Joe as soon as he entered the house why

Rusty had been disgruntled. Dagmar was yelling about the dog, Jack, in the house. She was lecturing Hannah and Ruth on temperance and the temptations of the flesh. Ruth calmly took Jack into the inner garden, where he happily chased the birds off the ground. Joe watched Hannah's face grow red, and stopped the woman in mid-sentence.

"Ma'am, you and your friends are welcome to spend the night in my home, but if you don't stop harassing my wife and mother, you'll find yourself sleeping under the stars without a blanket. We try to provide hot meals and comfortable beds for our guests. We don't expect rude and abusive behavior in return. Please restrain yourself." He gave her a fierce look, and the woman stared at him in shock. He supposed no man had stood up to her before.

"I'll have you know, young man, that we paid for our transportation to Denver, and I'm not in the habit of taking orders from males."

"Ma'am, until you learn to drive the coach and heft your own luggage into the boot, you'll have to accept the services of the men. Your tickets don't give you the right to lecture my wife. Now, enjoy your tea, take a walk around the grounds, or sit by the fireplace and read a book. We have work to do if you do not."

He turned as the older of the women, Lucile, he thought, placed her hand on Dagmar's sleeve. "Come, my dear, I would like to stretch my limbs. I think I saw a blue jay in the willow trees. I do delight in the colorful birds of nature, don't you?" And, with a great deal of effort, she drew Dagmar outside to stroll along the creek bed.

Gertrude remained within, and after a wink and smile, went to help Hannah clear the table of the dishes.

"I'm sorry, Mrs. Hadley. We aren't your enemies. It's a long ride, and the coach was stuffy and hot. She's not a bad woman, just determined. Please, tell me about the station. How long have you lived here?" Ruth came in, and the three women chatted of domestic matters, and Joe relaxed. But, he didn't go outside. He found a newspaper and pretended to read as he sat in the rocking chair, listening to the women. After a few minutes, the other women came back and went to their rooms. Two of the women, Lucile and Gertrude, were forced to occupy one bedroom, but Dagmar insisted on her own room. Hannah provided fresh water and clean flannel towels and left them.

Hannah served ham steaks, potatoes, turnips and peach cobbler. The men all trooped silently in and sat down to eat. Standing Tree took his usual place, and Dagmar stared at him. She opened her mouth, but saw Joe's glare and didn't speak. Gertrude made a comment about the weather; Lucile asked about the types of trees surrounding the station, and the men began to take part in the conversation at last. One, Jonathan Ford, was a botanist, and his associate was an artist, Reed Shelton. They had come to paint and record the flora and fauna of the mountains. Lucile became very interested, and Joe was able to direct the conversation to the beauty of the area and the red rock formations he had seen when hunting the wild mustangs.

During the meal, Jim Owens drove into the yard, two hours late, and lamented the loss of a horse that had gone lame. He had had to unhitch his mate, and use four horses for the remainder of the trip. The coach carried two miners, and with the addition of the men, the women were vastly outnumbered and withdrew to their bedrooms. The stage men went out to see to the animals, and Joe felt he could join them. Since they arrived so late, Jim and Fizzure threw their gear in the large room of the bunkhouse and went to sleep.

Before the sky had lightened with the glow of the sun, the coaches were prepared for departure, Jim and Fizzure back south, and Ivan and Hank with the passengers to Buckboard Station. All was quiet once more, and the residents returned to their chores. Peter went into the garden to pluck the produce for the women to can or cook; Joe had several dozen bricks drying in the sun; Slim was in the barn with the horses. With a few days left before the stage from Pueblo would return, Joe worked on the fireplace.

Late in the afternoon, Ivan and Hank returned with news of the great upheaval at Buckboard Station when the women arrived. Seeing the saloon in a portion of the Public Room, Dagmar had wielded her cane on the bottles and glasses with a mighty clatter of broken glass and spilled liquor. She harassed Bessie unmercifully and chased Shadrach Weaver from his home. She grabbed the ax from the wood pile and proceeded, with the help of her female friends, to destroy the Public Room itself. The male passengers were able to prevent the destruction of the manager's apartments, but the damage would take weeks to repair. Ivan and Hank, with the assistance of Shadrach, quickly hitched fresh horses to the coach and drove the women to Rockland Station, where they left them in the care of Moore and his wife, Jane.

Ivan saddled the sorrel stallion, Juno, and rode for miles to settle his troubled mind over the affair, and Hank set to work helping Joe build the fireplace. Peter came to join them, and Slim watered and fed grain and hay to the horses and set them free in the corral.

Joe finished the cabin roof and gave the bricks and mortar

of the fireplace a few days to dry before building a fire. He and Peter built shelves and placed pegs in the wall for hats and coats, and installed shutters for the windows. It was an impressive sight, sitting alone under the shade of the cottonwood tree, built on a solid foundation of river stones. Standing Tree watched the final construction and sat down beside the wall and lit his pipe. Joe watched as smoke began to curl around his head and laughed.

A few days later, Peter and Ruth moved into their cabin. The women cleaned their old room in preparation for guests on the route to Denver or to the south or east. A wagon train arrived from Denver with supplies for the winter. Peter planted the fall garden, and the root cellar was filled with jars of vegetables, and hanging from the ceiling were onions, garlic, peppers and other spices grown in the kitchen. The corn crib was full, and Hannah sat for hours grinding corn and wheat for flour.

Fuller was now walking with energy and was able to speak several complete sentences. Joe set him for the first time on a gentle saddle horse and rode him around the yard, to the laughter of the residents and barking of the dog, Jack. Standing Tree made him a suit of deerskin. He and Peter went to the river to fish for brown trout and catfish. The sun hovered overhead, hot and dry, and the men began to wish for rain. Slim seemed to withdraw from the family and spend more time alone working in the barn. Ivan and Hank passed the time between stages playing cards or reading the few books they had.

On returning from one trip, they told Joe and the others of the resignation of Shadrach Weaver and the placement of James Galbraith as the new manager of Buckboard Station, with his wife Belle, and three children. Joe and Hannah rode the next stage west to visit with them. Belle turned out to be a pleasant, middle-aged woman, Galbraith sober and friendly. The Public Room had been restored, and the saloon no longer occupied space in it.

About midday on a Saturday in late August, the brown coach from Pueblo pulled up and stopped just short of the new cabin. Tex climbed down from the box and stretched his arms and legs. From the opposite side of the coach, Mel opened the door, and two women stepped down, one primly dressed, and the other in a brightly decorated hat and carrying a closed parasol. They were traveling with their father, Yancy Charlton, to Cheyenne. He was a cattleman, he told them at supper, and his darling daughters were Mirabeth and Salacious, both experienced horsewomen. He was making plans to buy property on the plains west of Fort Laramie and start a new cattle range. If his plans went well, he'd drive a herd of steers to the place. With the coming of the railroad he'd be able to ship his cattle to the east for the people starving for meat after the war. Joe was fascinated by his plans. He said nothing, but it gave him an idea. He'd seen the cattle at Buckboard Station while visiting Galbraith.

Later, when the guests had gone to bed, he approached Peter with his idea. He'd never considered raising cattle before, but with the coming of the railroad and the change in the southern route of the stage, they might need a new food source. Standing Tree was getting older, and game would become scarce. Peter was skeptical at first, but the idea began to grow into a dream. They thought of where they could spread the cattle so they would have grazing and decided on the land between the station and the river, which he owned. If they felled some trees for fencing, leaving most of the timber for shade for the cattle, and cleaned out the underbrush, the cattle could roam at will, feed troughs could be built and they could even construct a shelter from the winter storms. The two men went to bed dreaming of things to be done.

Sixteen

When Slim was approached with the idea, he strongly objected and argued that he had enough to take care of already. Joe heard him out and suggested he take some time off in Denver. The idea of raising cattle was dropped and not spoken of again. Slim returned from Denver, more withdrawn than before, and in late September, he approached Joe with his plan. He had spoken with Tisdale while in Denver and asked for a transfer. He received a reply from Tisdale on the previous day's stage. Tisdale had explored the idea of setting up a clinic for him in Denver, where he would attend not only the animals of the stage line, but local clientele as well. Slim had accepted. A new animal handler would be coming within a few weeks. The rest of the week was spent in preparation for his departure. He replaced the shoes of those horses and mules that needed them, checked for wounds or abrasions, trimmed manes and tails, repaired harnesses and cleaned the barn surgery and forge area.

It was with a great deal of sadness and regret that Joe and Hannah said farewell to the animal handler. They had been through a lot together in the years of their association. On a bright, sunny day, early in the morning, Ivan and Hank pulled out and down the long forest road to Denver, with Slim Grimshaw and three other passengers aboard. There were tears in Hannah's eyes as she waved her white handkerchief. Ruth stood stiff and cool as she shook his hand. Joe watched until the stage disappeared and saddled Mack and went for a long ride with Standing Tree on the sorrel beside him, his bow and quiver of arrows on his back. They camped in the forest and returned three days later, the carcass of a deer on the back of Standing Tree's horse.

Joe plunged into the work of the station and played with his son when at leisure. Fall came early that year; the leaves turned color and fell from the trees; and red berries appeared on the vines and bushes. The chatter of ground squirrels was heard as they gathered seeds and nuts for the coming of winter. The stages came at regular intervals: Rusty and Grover from the east, Owens and Rodriguez from Trinidad, Tex and Mel from Pueblo. The passengers came in a procession of style, character, demeanor and personalities, and went about their business here and there, with hardly a remembrance left behind them. The new animal handler didn't arrive, and Joe was left with the care of the animals with the help of Peter and the coachmen.

The United States Mail pouch was lifted from the front boot, examined for letters for the residents and passed on to the next station. Joe was surprised to receive a letter from Claude Edison, Hannah's uncle. It was a cheerful letter full of news, and he and his family peered over it with mixed emotions. Claudette and Margaret were both married, Claudette to a merchant in town, and now the mother of a boy, Thaddeus. Margaret had married a farmer and was living several miles away. He wrote of several of the neighbors the Hadleys had

193

known; they had joined a new church congregation and were pleased with the minister. They had recently made a trip to Indianapolis and enjoyed the museums and theater. He hoped Hannah was well, and he also extended the same wish for Joe's parents. He asked for news of his niece and family: Sincerely, Claude Edison, Greenwood, Indiana.

The family sat near the fireplace long into the night, talking about the past and the neighbors they had known. Joe wrote a note telling Claude something of the station and their life in Colorado. It was sent out on the next stage. No mention was made about his brother, Luther Hadley, still living at the home farm, as far as Joe knew, in either letter.

The stages stopped running on schedule in late October as the harsh weather set in, with snow and ice, and cold, brisk winds from the north. Wolves were heard howling in the forest, but didn't approach the buildings. Peter and Ruth moved back into the big house, since it took too much wood for three fireplaces, and it was hard for Ruth to walk in the ice and snow. Joe began to read from a book to Fuller, and his finger would point to the words with glee. Standing Tree slept in one of the bunkhouse rooms on the floor. Hannah made a quilt and cooked for the family. Ruth caught a bad cold and spent the greater part of a week in bed, but recovered with a cough that kept Peter worried during the night.

Joe was out every day with the animals, with the help of Ivan, Hank and Peter. When the days were sunny, he went into the forest for fallen limbs and brought them back for firewood. The first of November appeared mild, and everyone was surprised to see a farm wagon pull up to the door. It was the animal handler, Roland Abernathy, with his ten-year-old son, Bub, short for Walter. He explained he'd stayed in town because his sister had been ill. She was now recovered from her illness, and engaged in caring for her large family.

He brought supplies from Tisdale: foodstuffs, books and magazines, board games, and clothing for the station members. The stage agent said to keep the wagon and four horses at the station until he decided what to do with them. The men separated the items and put the food in the shed or root cellar, and the other things were brought into the house to be distributed among the members. Joe fell on the books with joy; he handed a few to be put in the bunkhouse and drew a new pair of boots on his feet with pleasure. There were trousers and boots for the men, shoes for the women and heavy wool coats for all. Joe laughed, for he was wearing the coat he'd received from Israel Bodkin, the tailor in Denver.

It was like having Christmas a month early; they were so pleased to see the supplies. And, Betty had not forgotten Fuller. There was a rubber ball, a bag of marbles and a wooden train, with wheels, an engine, four cars, and a caboose, carved by an expert carpenter. There was no track, but the boy pulled the string, and the train followed him until he yanked too hard and it fell on its side. Whoever was close by would right the cars until he learned to do it himself.

Joe hadn't expected a boy with his handler, but Roland agreed to keep him with him in the bunkhouse. He settled in, met the other residents and walked around the barn and corrals, while Hannah fed Bub some pie and milk. Joe parked the wagon beside the barn and kept the animals in the barn until he was satisfied they would blend well with the other animals. They were branded with the mark of the stage line and looked to be in good health. The weather stayed warm for two more days, and a blizzard blew in; and the residents were shut in for days.

November changed to December and advanced into a cold, dark January. Limbs fell from several trees in the forest; the spring froze over, and Hank tried some ice skating without skates and fell on his rump and laughed. He picked himself up and challenged the others to try, Roland and his son ventured cautiously onto the ice and stayed on their feet. A thaw appeared, and Joe decided it was too dangerous to spend time on the ice, so they ran a foot race instead. They all gathered in the Public Room for hot coffee and cake.

Roland proved to be as efficient and skilled with the animals as Slim, but without the medical qualifications. He'd learned his skills with experience and hard labor. It soon came out that his wife had died in childbirth, and he sorely missed her. Her name was Addie. At first, he was hesitant to speak of her, but with a little coaxing he elaborated on his background, something Slim had never done through the years. He was a farmer from Ohio, whose parents had come from Ireland. His wife had been a neighbor, and they had married young. Bub proved to be a good rider and obedient. He helped bring in water and firewood without grumbling. He ventured out one pleasantly warm evening when Peter and Standing Tree were smoking under the cottonwood and started asking questions a curious boy of ten would ask. They took him under their wings, and they became good friends. He remained reserved when Joe was around.

The stage and mail delivery were sketchy during February because of the erratic weather; mostly single men going to Denver. A few risked the road south to Pueblo, but the northbound from Trinidad only ran twice. Joe and Hannah were pleased to receive a letter from Matthew Baldwin, telling them he was well and happy. The stage route wasn't too difficult and the horses well trained. He said his sister Gladys had been delivered of a baby boy, and he was an uncle. All the family was well the last time he had heard from them. He gave an address where he could be reached, and Joe promptly wrote him back.

In early March, the residents were called to attention by the sound of Rusty's blaring trumpet. The boy was especially excited and ran to see the coach come to a stop near the small cabin.

"Hello, the house. Where the hell is everyone?" Rusty stared down at the young boy, and climbed down from the box. Grover moved more slowly, his own eyes drawn to the lad standing with wide eyes looking at them. "Howdy, young'un. Where's Joe?"

Joe came running from the barn where he'd been helping Roland with a mare about to give birth. He stopped dead in his tracks as Rusty opened the door of the coach, and two women stepped down, followed by four men. The first woman wore lavender with a black coat, gloves and hat. The second had on dark blue with a fur coat of brown and fur hat to match the coat. Two gentlemen were dressed as merchants, and the other two as farmers.

"Hello." He came out of his trance. "Howdy, Rusty. Haven't seen you in a spell. How's the sand bogs? Are they drying up from the rain last week?" He turned to the visitors. "Welcome to Sweetwater Station. We weren't expecting company. Please come in out of the cold. Dinner's on the stove." He expected an introduction from Rusty or Grover but received none, so led the guests to the Public Room, followed by Bub. He saw Roland come to take the head of the mules and nodded his satisfaction before entering the house. Rusty and Grover were left to themselves with the new animal handler. The two merchants and one other man went into the house. The other man, a tall, slender chap in denims and linen shirt stayed outside, looking around him. Joe saw Ivan and Hank come out of the bunkhouse to greet their fellow coachmen.

Joe put his hat on the peg and turned to the guests. "Hello, I'm Joe Hadley, and this is my wife, Hannah, and my mother, Ruth. Please be seated, while the ladies get the meal on the table." Hannah looked at the guests with surprise and reached for the cups. Ruth grabbed a cloth and turned with the coffee pot. They hadn't expected visitors, but always kept coffee for the residents on cold days. Hannah stirred her pot of beans and brought it to the table. She lifted the cloth from the basket of freshly baked bread. Ruth set plates and utensils on the table, adding a jar of pickles in the middle. She went to the cellar for some goat cheese. Hannah sliced a couple of onions for relish. There was rice and cabbage. There was half an apple pie left, and she put that on the table and sliced it into wedges. Ruth brought some johnnycakes, hot from the stove.

"Good day," replied one of the men; the taller one. "I'm Jesse Wingold from Minnesota, and this is my wife Laurel, my brother Royce and his wife Peggy. We're on our way to Pueblo. We were told we can transfer here to another stage. The agent said we might have to wait a bit for the weather to clear. Do you have accommodations for us to stay until the stage gets here?" He laid his hat on the floor beside the table and shed his coat and gloves. Joe took the ladies' wraps and hung them on pegs. The single man dropped onto a chair with his hat and coat still on. He gulped the coffee down with a sly look toward Hannah's face. He stood and filled his plate with beans and took a couple of slices of bread from the basket without waiting for the ladies.

Joe watched Ruth serve the ladies a plate of beans and wedge of cheese. He turned to answer the man's question.

"I don't know when the coach will arrive out of Pueblo; depends on the road conditions. We have rooms available. What's your business in Pueblo, if you don't mind saying?" Joe sat and took a sip of his coffee. When Ruth had refilled the cups, she went to the boys and said something to Bub, and picked up Fuller and brought him to his chair. Bub sat quietly at the table listening to the conversation.

"We sell general merchandise. We have an aunt who lives in Pueblo, wife of one of the lawyers in town. She wrote it was a growing town. Her husband found a large building and a couple of houses for us. We decided to come; have a look around before we make the giant leap forward. You know anything about the town?" Jesse finished his coffee and sat back with a sigh. Joe could see no physical resemblance between the brothers, except a general appearance, Royce being shorter and heavier set, and with gray eyes.

"Just what I've heard. We've never been there. It's on the Arkansas River; a lot of trade with the Cheyenne Indian village nearby. The stage has only stopped here since last year. It used to go to Mozier Station, which you left this morning."

The brother spoke up. "We read in the newspaper there was a stage coach robbery hereabouts. And, occasionally Indian trouble. I voted against this venture, but Jesse is a stubborn man. That true about the coach robbery?" He paused with a spoonful of beans in his hand. Both of the women looked up, eyes wide with curiosity. Ruth fed Fuller a bite of biscuit. He banged on the table with his spoon.

"Quiet, son." Joe took the spoon from his son's hand. The boy looked at his father, and Ruth gave him another piece of bread, which he stuffed in his mouth with one fist. She fed him some beans, and put four wooden blocks on the table for him to stack. Joe turned to the men. "Yes, it's true about the robbery. Several men and a lady were killed. The posse chased them for days, but didn't find any trace. The marshal figured they headed on west into the mountains. There's been no Indian trouble since we've been here." He watched as Hannah went into the root cellar and came back with a large bowl of potatoes. She picked up a knife and began to peel the potatoes. Ruth was helping Fuller stack his blocks. Occasionally, he opened his mouth for more beans or bread.

The single man turned to Joe. "Hadley, my name's Gibson. I'm on my way north to homestead in Utah or Montana, if I can find land. We've read that it's good cattle country. Large rolling plains and plentiful grass. Wide open skies and large forests near the mountains. I have a contact in Denver who says that's so. I've come to talk with him. But, I'm concerned about the Indian situation." He took off his hat and laid it on the floor. He had apparently finished his meal, as he pushed the plate away.

"I don't know anything about Utah or Montana, but I've heard there's good grassland west of Fort Laramie northwest of here in Wyoming Territory. The Indians hereabouts are friendly. Mostly Arapahoe and Bannack. Directly north I've heard the Sioux and Crow are fierce tribes, resentful of the white men. The Comanche and Kiowa were active near Fort Dodge south of here a couple of years back. The Army lost several men, I heard, and had their horses stolen. I'd suggest, if it were me, go on to Oregon or Idaho. My friend is of the Arapahoe tribe." He turned to Bub. "Go get Standing Tree, son." The boy left the house with a grin on his face.

Joe sat and sipped his coffee, while he observed the other

men. They were looking around the room; Gibson was staring at Hannah's scarred face. He saw Joe's eyes observing him and picked up his cup and drank from it. Ruth asked if the ladies would like to go to their rooms. They accepted the invitation and left the room. The door opened, and Standing Tree came in, with Bub cautiously stepping to the side. He watched the men with curious eyes.

Joe rose. "This is my friend, Standing Tree." He turned and signed and spoke in the few words he knew about the area north of Fort Laramie called Montana. "Good land? Good for growing animals with horns called cattle? Peaceful Indians? Many white men live on land?"

Standing Tree looked at the strangers with his assessing black eyes. He shook his head. "Strong Indians; heap trouble. White soldiers too many. Trouble come by and by, if white man come. Buffalo go away; animals with horns eat grass of buffalo. Indian grow angry, kill white man, maybe." He pulled his blanket tight around his body and sat down. Hannah handed him a glass of water. He reached for an onion and chewed it slowly. And, burped. She filled his plate with beans, and he started eating. His gaze lifted often to the boy, Fuller.

Joe watched the reaction of the men; one seemed resigned; one curious and the leader, Wingold, angry. "Well, there it is. Talk to your friend in Denver; but I'd advise you to stay clear of the area. Now, if you've finished your meal, I'll show you the grounds and the bunkhouse. I have to get the mules ready for the return to Mozier Station." He started across the floor to get his hat but heard a wail from Fuller. He saw he had knocked down his tower of blocks. Bub was trying to stack them again, but Fuller knocked them back down with his fist. Joe settled the dispute by lifting Fuller from the chair, taking him to the play area and whispering in his ear. He saw that the men had left the building.

He went to Hannah and gave her a friendly pat on the shoulder. "Have you enough food, dear? I didn't expect a stage so soon. I wonder if Jim or Tex will come since the weather is mild."

"If you'll bring in some bacon for breakfast, we've enough. I don't have any dessert baked. I guess I better get started on that." She sighed and smiled at Standing Tree. She peeled a stretch of rind off the potato in her hand. "I'll put on more beans, but they won't get done by supper. I can make soup, instead. We'll manage; go on and take care of the outside business."

"Fine. If you need anything else send Bub out for me. Come on, my friend." He left with Standing Tree following, and found the man in the denims and linen shirt at the coach. He seemed to be arguing with Rusty.

"No, sir, Powell. I don't go no further than this station. If you want to go on tonight, you'll have to talk to Joe or Ivan. Me and Grover are headed back to Mozier, soon's the team's changed." Rusty put his cigar in his mouth, drew several puffs and turned to Joe. "I'm going to the house for coffee, Joe." He took off as fast as his old legs would travel. Grover was over by the corrals, his shotgun still on his shoulder talking with Roland. He appeared to be relaxed, but Joe knew he could hear the conversation.

"What seems to be the trouble, Powell?" Joe saw that Roland had moved to the forge area with one of the mules, Grover came to take the luggage from the stage and Ivan and Hank had disappeared.

"No trouble. Just inquiring about the rest of the way to

202

Denver. I'd like to go on tonight, but the driver says we have to stay here." He frowned and kicked the dirt with frustration. He had a rugged face and broad shoulders. His clothes were wrinkled and dusty. There was a pistol in the leather holster on his hip.

"He's right. Ivan Mandrake will be taking you to Buckboard Station in the morning. It's best to give the ladies a night in a bed along the route, as they tire easily. Besides, this is the first run of the week. We have to wait to see if the northbound stage comes through this afternoon. You should go eat your dinner, and there are board games, books and things in the large room of the bunkhouse to entertain you while you wait."

"There's no chance of going on tonight? Damn. I've been on the road three days. Should have taken the train." He looked at the distant mountains, covered in clouds. "Is this the place that had the robbery last year? I read about it in the papers."

"A few miles south of here." He dismissed it as unimportant. "Go on and eat your meal; I have work to do."

The man grunted a reply and went into the house. Joe turned to Grover. "What's all that about? The man inside asked about the robbery, too. But, both say they're going north. That fellow looks nervous." He lifted the last piece of baggage from the boot, a square box, with lettering that said, "Sweetwater Station, Colorado Territory." Curious, he set it on the ground.

"Where'd this come from?" He drew his finger along the lettering.

"Came with the mail pouch. Mail's been stacking up since we've been delayed because of the weather. Thanks for the help, Joe. I'm going in to eat.' He and Joe took the luggage to the porch and set it down, to be sorted later, and Grover went inside.

Joe went to help Roland hitch the mules to the coach. He took off his hat and gazed at the distant mountains. He noticed Standing Tree sitting under the tree, smoking. He wiped the grime from his face and put his hat back on. "One of those men seems to be looking for trouble. He's in an awful hurry to get to Denver. Help me keep an eye on him. His name's Powell. He and Gibson will stay in the bunkhouse."

Roland turned and spoke. "I noticed that. I've been thinking, if the westbound got through, the northbound probably will, too. They don't have that patch of sand bogs to come through. I've selected the horses, just in case."

"That's fine. Let's get these mules hitched, and you can take time to eat, while I watch them. Heh, Bub." He turned to the boy as he came from the house. "Come help us with the mules. You're old enough to learn the process."

When the mules were hitched, Roland and his son went to the house. He and Bub lifted the luggage and the box and took them into the house. Ivan came from the bunkhouse.

"I don't like the looks of those clouds, Joe. You think we're in for a storm?" Ivan went to the coach and opened the door. "Damn, one of the ladies has left her handbag behind." He drew it out and showed it to Joe. It was a dainty black velvet affair with a metal opening and chain. He could feel the shape of a small caliber pistol. He didn't open it but took off to the house. "I'll be back."

Joe watched him go and looked again at the mountain peaks covered with heavy dark clouds. He went to the bunkhouse and knocked on Hank's door. There was no answer. He went down the hallway and found the man reading a book.

"It looks like a build-up to a storm. I don't think it'll come for a while. Help us get the chickens and goats into their shelter.

I'll tell Rusty, see if he wants to get on the road, or wait until morning." He crossed to the house. Standing Tree followed him inside and sat down by the fireplace.

"Rusty, better swallow your food and get on the road if you're going. It looks like rain coming from the mountains. Maybe tonight by the looks of it. Or, we could tie the coach down and put the animals in the sheds." He didn't finish, because Rusty and Grover were on their feet, and the guard grabbed his shotgun and hat. He had a piece of bread in his hand. He stuffed it in his mouth and cursed. Rusty stopped at the coach.

"It's a long way off. We'll make a run for it. Hurry, Joe and check the axles and wheels." He went to the leader of the team and within minutes, the coach was on the road east, leaving several worried people behind.

Joe and Roland, Peter and Ivan, Hank and the new man, Gibson, put the chickens in the coop and the goats in their shed. They were moving the horses and mules into sheds and barn, when a great bellow was heard, and Jim Owens drove into the yard with Fizzure aboard the high seat. Jim jumped down and opened the door. A lady dressed all in black and a small girl and boy trailed into the house after her. Three men stepped down and followed them into the house.

"Jim, it looks like a storm's coming; I just sent Rusty on his way; but I don't think you should try to move on tonight. Move the coach next to the bunkhouse, and we'll tie it down. There's room in the barn for a few more horses. You'll have to double up in the rooms; we have a house full of people already."

Jim looked at the clouds and pulled the coach as close to the building as it would go without scratching the surface. Fizzure and Ivan got ropes from the supply room in the barn and tied it securely to a tree. Roland and Bub moved the horses into shelter under a couple of sheds. Joe cursed under his breath. He had a full house, sheds and barn. Peter and Ruth would be in their small cabin; the two ladies with husbands would have the rooms on the left side hallway; and the lady with her two children in the room next to Joe and Hannah. If he had to, he and Hannah could bunk out in his parents' place and give their room to some guests. The eight rooms and large room of the bunkhouse would be full of single men.

Jim and Fizzure went to eat their meal, and Joe and Roland checked out the horses that had just arrived, looking for cuts, scrapes or harness burns. Satisfied that they were good, he finally went in to eat his own meal. There was very little; a bit of bread; a few beans, but he made do with a hunk of cheese and coffee. He looked at Hannah, who had a frown on her face. Ruth was busy at the stove, stirring a pot. Joe finished and looked around him. The Public Room was full of people: the coachmen were at the table, eating; Jesse Wingold was reading the papers from Denver; four of the men were playing cards. The three ladies were sitting on the sofa and rocking chair talking. The two visiting children were playing with Fuller on the floor.

Joe cleared his throat. "People, it looks like a storm is coming from over the mountains. We have a full house tonight. I've seen these heavy storms before, with thunder, lightning, hail, rain, limbs falling from the trees and pine cones littering the ground. We've put the animals in shelters and tied down the coaches. It's the best we can do outside. The next thing is to house you people. Those of you who have assigned rooms should be safe with the shutters drawn tight; you single men will be in the bunkhouse; those who haven't individual rooms can stay in the large room. There are plenty of blankets and quilts, pillows and lamps, and lanterns and firewood. The important thing is don't panic and go out in the storm, once it commences to start. Choose either your assigned place or stay here; but don't try to go out in the rain. There are books, magazines, board games to entertain; plenty of food and water. I think it'll hit around sunset or later, so if there's anything that needs doing, do it now. That's all."

The room was instant bedlam; men clambering for attention; the women frightened; the children ran to their mother; and all the while, Hannah stirred her pot of soup, and Ruth helped Fuller with his blocks. Everyone finally settled down, and a few of the men went to the bunkhouse with supplies to cook their own meal in the fireplace, if necessary.

Peter and Ruth agreed to stay for a while until the wind picked up or the rain fell. One of the ladies, Peggy Wingold, asked what she could do to help with dinner, and the three ladies, peeled, scraped, fried, and pulled two apple pies and fresh loaves of bread from the oven. Laurel Wingold stayed in her room, while her husband played poker with some other men in the bunkhouse. Powell complained about the inconvenience, but was distracted by Peter who started a conversation about the possibility of raising cattle in the plains of Montana. Gibson joined in, and the talk drifted to other subjects.

Joe and Roland, accompanied by Bub, Fizzure and Ivan checked on the animals and the coaches. The clouds were huge, white and round as they rose high in the sky, and the mountains disappeared in a purplish-gray haze. Joe looked to the forest, and it seemed dark and gloomy. The trees were absolutely still; no birds were heard in their branches. He walked along the fence line to see if there were any downed logs, and the dog walked along beside him. It was so still, the air oppressive, and he smelled the smoke from the chimneys. It seemed to rise straight into the sky.

He heard a sound and gazed at Fizzure, with his shotgun on his shoulder, looking towards the forest. Joe walked over to him.

"Do you see something?"

"No. That's what worries me. It's too quiet, Joe. No animals or birds stirring. No sound in the trees." He started walking toward Standing Tree, sitting under his tree, his eyes looking at the house.

"What say you, Injun? Big storm? Much hail, rain from Big Father in the Sky?" For the first time since Joe had known him, Fizzure broke into a language of his own. He held his shotgun in the bend of his elbow while he made sign. He turned to Joe.

"He senses it, Joe. Says it will come about sunset, with great winds and hunks of ice from the sky. I can feel it in my bones; we're in for trouble. You should have kept Rusty and Grover here. I hope they make to Mozier."

"They left early, should get there before it hits that station. What do you think? Buckboard? I wish we had some way to warn them of the danger." He included Standing Tree in his suppositions.

"Yo Hadley wait. Big storm blow soon." The Indian took his pipe from his pocket and lit it. Fizzure squatted beside him and took a cigar from his pocket. They sat smoking, and Joe left them to see about the animals again. He walked the length of the barn and looked in the stall where his stallion Mack stood restless and stomping the dirt floor with his hoof.

"You sense it too, don't you, big fellow? It'll be alright. You're safe in here. I built the walls to stand; it's the roof that might cave in." He gave the horse a piece of apple, and went to the next stall. One by one, he went down the line and out to the sheds. He heard a sound and looked around; it was the man Gibson.

"I was talking to your father. He said you're from Indiana. Around Greenwood? I came from a small town about fifty miles north of Indianapolis. Were you in the war?" He didn't seem tense, and Joe answered truthfully.

"Yes, Confederate, Morgan's troops. Lots of good Indiana men died."

"That's a fact. I joined up when they first came to town asking for men. Union troops. Got back from the fighting and wasn't able to settle, so I lit out for Texas. Caught a steamer and went to New Orleans and moved on to Galveston." He scratched his chest. "Guess I wanted to get as far from the battles as I could. You feel the same?" He leaned against the wall and seemed to be ready to stay a spell.

Joe looked around and saw that the dust was being stirred. The tree tops were moving. He couldn't see the mountains, but the clouds were no longer round and puffy, but spread over the sky in gray and white pillows, jumbled and moving along the edges. A few patches of blue could still be seen between the clouds.

"Yes. That's why I took the position as manager. Had night-mares for the first year or so. They've tapered off some, but I still wake up in the middle of the night thinking of those days. I've been here nigh on five years. My son was born in that house. Saw a few deaths, too." He pointed to the mounds among the towering pine trees north of the spring. Thoughtfully, he gazed at the sky. "Look at those clouds, straight as an arrow across the horizon." He was silent for so long, he jumped when

Gibson began to speak again.

"I stayed south for a couple of years and herded cattle for a while. Interesting animals, cattle. Lazy critters, stand around eating grass all day, but let a leaf or rodent come within sight, and they take off on a run. I saved my money and decided to head north and buy my own spread."

"There's a small herd of cattle at Buckboard Station, on the west. You'll be there tomorrow if the storm is over so the coach can travel. Freighters brought them out years ago. The stage agent had the idea that the wild game will disappear once the settlers start building houses and towns. I thought once of getting a few head and a bull, but my animal handler at the time wasn't encouraging. Takes a full time hand, he said." He shrugged and toed the ground with his boot. He hated to think of the way Slim had left them.

"Is that right? You wanted to herd cattle here?" Gibson looked around at the whole picture, and settled on the long grassy area toward the river to the southwest. "You could do it, Hadley. Down that way, looks like good grass." He turned and gazed at Joe. "But, I suppose this is stage line property. You'd have to consider that angle, but if there's cattle at the next station, they probably wouldn't care if you have a small herd, say five to ten cows and a bull. No great herd. Too many trees. I don't mind eating venison and pork, but give me a good beef steak anytime. What do you say? You want me to talk to the station manager at Buckboard, see if he'd sell a few head?"

Joe looked at Gibson as though he'd grown horns. Could he? Should he? He remembered talking to his father, but Slim had been so adamant.

"Well, I'd better think about it. As you say, ask permission from the stage agent in Denver. But, thanks for the offer. I'll write a letter and send it in the mail going out tomorrow. Right now, I got this storm to think on. And, look at that dust blow. You go to the bunkhouse and give the men a warning. I want to check on a horse in the barn." He was on the run to the barn before his words stopped echoing around the yard. He found Roland with the mare and the new-born colt, just beginning to stand on his feet. He grinned. It gave him a thrill every time a new horse or mule was born from the feral horses he had caught among the mountain gullies and boulders to the northwest of the station. It reminded him of John Dempsey and his first day as a station manager.

"Everything going well? You'd best get ready; the wind's kicking up something fierce. Stay in the barn; the walls are snug and tight; can't say about the roof, but it's held so far. You'll have to handle anything alone. Or, I could send Papa out, if you think you need help." He frowned.

"No. You take care of the guests. I'll be fine here. I want to stay with the mare until I'm sure she's recovered from her ordeal." With a wave, he turned back to the colt. "I think I'll call him Stormy." Joe laughed and left the barn to run to the house. The wind was swift, and he had to hold his hand over his mouth to breathe. He took a quick look and saw no one outside.

Seventeen

Inside the house, nothing much had changed since he'd left. It was dark with shadows on the walls since the shutters were closed down tight. Lanterns glowed on the fireplace mantle; the table lamps were filled and burning brightly. The kitchen area was lighted from lanterns and flickering candles. Fuller was playing with his tiny metal soldiers. The older children were on the floor in front of the blazing fireplace, playing a board game. Standing Tree was watching them from a spot near the wall, the dog asleep beside him. Laurel Wingold was still in her room; Peggy was helping Hannah and Ruth prepare the evening meal. Emma Summers was sitting in a straight back chair repairing a rent in her son's trousers, while keeping an eye on the children.

The men were talking to Jim and Peter about farming methods and speculation whether the price of wheat and oats would rise or fall that year. Joe joined them and heard the wind begin to whistle around the eaves of the house. A few of the guests looked up but seemed calm. Laurel came from the bedroom, looking sleepy and her clothes rumpled. She sat at the table and watched the other women working. Her sister-in-law handed her a loaf of bread and a knife. She blinked and stood to slice the bread.

A roaring sound was heard outside, and Joe watched the reactions of the guests. The conversations stopped and then continued. Rain began to fall on the roof, and within minutes there was the unmistakable sound of hail. Jack began to bark, and the children rose to run around the room, until Royse told them to sit down. Joe pulled the excited dog into his arms and listened to the wind and rain. Occasionally, someone would exclaim at a particularly loud boom of thunder, but the lightning couldn't be seen because of the closed windows and doors. On and on it droned, then suddenly the hail stopped, and only the gentle rain could be heard. The adults rose to feed their children and put them to bed.

Hannah called out that supper was ready, and the chairs were brought to the table and every seat was taken. Coffee cups and water glasses were filled; a couple of the ladies chose milk. Royce looked at Standing Tree but didn't speak to him. Bread was passed around; likewise, a platter of pickles, cheese wedges, pickled beets and onions. The soup was ladled into bowls; the meat was sliced thin and tasty; the vegetables went around to those who chose to eat them. Finally, slices of hot apple pie and spice cake were served, and the guests withdrew from the table to sit again around the fireplace to discuss recent events; some told personal stories and a few jokes were properly received with laughter.

Nearly ten of the clock, Emma Summers declared with a genteel yawn that she must go to her children. Laurel crossed the room and moved down the hallway to her room, but Peggy stayed to help with the dishes. Standing Tree stretched out on the floor and went to sleep. The conversation sank into

213

whispers, and Royce and Peggy went to their room. Peter and Ruth covered their heads with newspapers and dashed out into the rain. Joe watched them to their door and turned to Gibson and Powell with a broad hint that it was time to turn in. He saw them safely to the bunkhouse and drew a deep breath of relief. The rain was coming down in a gentle mist; the ground was wet with puddles in places near the house. Last of all, Jim Owens, after a nod to Hannah, left for the bunkhouse. Joe shooed Jack out for a last tramp in the rain, and when he returned, he closed the door and locked it.

He blew out the candles, lamps and lanterns but one, and he and Hannah went to their own room. He was exhausted and knew that Hannah was, too. They lay quietly talking for a while, and finally slept while the rain continued to fall on the buildings among the pine tree forest.

When Hannah awoke and opened the front door, the sun was awakening to a new day. The air was fresh and clear. A few late stars still shone, and the buildings stood in shadows. She started a fire in the stove and was startled when Standing Tree rose and came to the table.

"Scarred Woman work too much. White man go soon. Yo Hadley tell people go from place of home. Big wagon with box take away. Far away to north wind, I think. I hungry."

He sat down, and Hannah gave him a glass of water. She went to the larder and brought back the slab of bacon and began to slice it thinly. She had a few eggs and brought out her small skillet and cooked two. He drank the water, ate the eggs and waited for the rest. Joe stumbled into the room with the boy, still half asleep. He put him, still in his nightshirt, in the tall chair. His cheeks were streaked with tears.

"Yo Hadley tell people go from this place. Scarred Woman

make cook soon; she sit down. He cook." He pointed a long, pale finger at Joe and signed for him to hear him speak.

"What? What's he saying, Hannah?" He looked around the room and sat down.

"I think he's telling you to cook breakfast, honey."

Joe stared at Standing Tree, and shaking his head, he got up and told Hannah to sit. She sat beside Fuller's chair and sighed.

Joe clumsily cooked the bacon and put a pot of water on for porridge, with Hannah's instructions. The coffee began to perk, and he poured two cups, took a sip and grinned. It was stronger than usual. Hannah fed the boy a soft yellow egg and cautioned Joe to stir the porridge or it would burn. They all turned when they heard Peter and Ruth come in. Their eyes grew wide in amazement when they saw Hannah and Standing Tree sitting and Joe cooking breakfast.

Peter had the milk bucket in his hands. Ruth went to the stove and rescued the pot of porridge from the fire. She collected the tins in preparation for making biscuits. Joe put the bacon on a plate and handed it to Hannah, and ladled some porridge into her bowl. He poured a cup of milk for her and the boy.

Peter took the hint and strained the milk of insects. He poured his own coffee while Joe put more bacon into the skillet. Ruth finished the dough and put two large pans of biscuits into the oven. She sat down and ate her own eggs and bacon. Joe finished that mess of bacon and started more, while the aroma of fresh bread permeated the air. He plucked a slice of bacon from the plate and put it in his mouth and chewed.

Standing Tree, satisfied that things were going the way he wanted, finished his porridge and water and went outside, gathering his blanket around him against the cool air. The four adults left behind looked at each other, and Hannah explained to Peter and Ruth what had happened. Ivan and Hank came in, and soon, Royse Wingold entered the Public Room. By this time, the biscuits were done, with more in the oven. Joe, Ivan and Hank left to go to the coach and animals. The horses were hitched. Ivan drove the black coach out of its shed, and Joe and Hank untied the ropes from the brown coach from Trinidad. Horses were hitched, and they began their inspections of the vehicles and animals.

There were a few limbs down, and pools of water stood in wheel ruts and holes. A shutter was missing from a window of the bunkhouse. Joe looked to the creek, but it didn't look past its banks. When Roland came from the bunkhouse, he rode one of the saddle horses bareback to check further up the creek. There were small limbs and trash along the banks, but he was certain the coaches could get safely across. He left the saddle horse tied to a corral post and went back to the barn to check on the new mother and her colt.

With a flurry of skirts and shouted good-byes, Emma and her two children stepped into the black coach, followed by Gibson and Powell. Ivan climbed aboard, and they were soon on their way to Buckboard Station. Jim and Fizzure started on their journey to Trinidad, and the only remaining guests were the Wingold brothers and their wives. The sun rapidly warmed the atmosphere, and the water receded from the puddles. In the afternoon, Joe built a fire in the pit, and the old wash tub was brought out. Soon, clothing and bedding were washed and hung on the lines. Peggy helped with supper, while Laurel read a book. The men devoured the few newspapers available, and as the sun was passing behind the forest road, Ivan and Hank appeared with news and two passengers on the way to Pueblo, named Ida Mae Payne and her husband, George. Payne was a dentist and Ida a jolly, heavy-set matron with gray hair set atop her head in braids.

Buckboard Station had been hit hard. There was damage to the house, and the barn had flooded; a couple of chickens drowned, and the animal handler's arm was broken when he slipped on the muddy ground. Gibson decided to stay and help them recover. Galbraith and Belle were well but had a lot of work to do to recover from the storm. The men whiled away the rest of the day in small talk, and Ida helped with the kitchen chores.

Joe cut the fallen limbs for firewood while Ivan and Hank cleaned the mud off the coach with Bub's help. Roland tended to the livestock, and Peter repaired the shutter on the bunkhouse. The sun left the sky in a blaze of color and tinted the tops of the faraway snow-topped mountains.

The next day, right on schedule, Tex and Mel drove into the yard, and after a meal of ham, potatoes, fried onions and cornbread whisked the remaining visitors to the south. Hannah and Ruth waved good-bye from the porch and returned to the kitchen for a soothing cup of tea. The bedrooms in the house and the bunkhouse were turned out and cleaned, and the bedclothes were lined up in the yard, where they flapped and snapped in the breeze. Standing tree and Peter mounted horses and went fishing. Roland spent the afternoon at the forge giving a couple of horses new shoes, with his son helping him.

It wasn't until all the guests had left that Joe remembered the box sent with the mail pouch. He opened it and sat back on his heels in dismay at the contents. He called Hannah and his parents, and they went through the items one by one. It was accompanied on top by a letter from Luther's wife, Sadie.

217

Luther Hadley had been killed by a fire in the barn, trying to rescue the horses and milk cow. She had moved to Indianapolis with the cook and housekeeper. The land and buildings had been sold. There was enclosed a cashier's check on a Denver bank, in the name of Peter Hadley.

Inside the box, covered with a thin India rubber sheet to keep them dry, and carefully wrapped in old newspapers, were Ruth's delicate glass figurine collection and pictures. There were the tintypes of James in his Union uniform; and Joe in Confederate gray. Faded letters and documents filled part of the space, and there was a walnut box holding Saul Hadley's dueling pistols. The women burst into tears, as Joe and Peter sat, stunned but delighted. The box was put away until Joe could make a curio cabinet for the collection of cherished family heirlooms.

Joe and Hank, with Ivan driving the farm wagon with tools and split logs, rode the saddle horses along the fence line, looking for damage, and repaired it when it was found. They hauled several fallen limbs and branches back to be cut into firewood. The next day, with the ground thoroughly dry, he used the scythe to cut the tall grass for hay for the animals. Everything was back to normal, and the new colt called Stormy was brought out of the barn and led around the yard to the delight of Hannah and Fuller, who clapped his hands and chortled his approval; its mother trailed behind bawling for her youngster. Roland took them back to the barn, until the colt was old enough to be weaned. Standing Tree sat under his tree, smoking his pipe, his black eyes watching in silence.

Joe was amazed when Gibson and the animal handler from Buckboard rode into the station yard with a herd of five cows and a bull named Trudo. Galbraith had sent them over; said he had more than he could take care of, what with the damage to the station. They were driven onto the meadow between the creek and the river and allowed to roam at will. Gibson gave Joe a few tips on how to care for them, and he and the handler returned to Buckboard. He told Joe he would be on his way to Montana as soon as the repairs were made. Joe shook his hand and wished him well in his new adventure.

The next day, a mule was born, and Roland was busy in the barn. Joe finished cutting the grass around the spring and along the creek bank. The hay was piled high in neat stacks, to be baled with cords, and stored in the barn. Peter worked in the garden. Root vegetables were planted and corn harvested in the field across the creek. The stages ran on schedule, and the guests came and went with hardly a notice.

May and June flowed into a bright, hot July afternoon, when Wallace Tisdale arrived on the eastbound stage, accompanied by three newly hired outriders. It wasn't good. He took Joe aside and talked for a long time. All the eastern stage stations including Mozier were being closed. The properties were sold and the animals would be auctioned off to the highest bidder. With the joining of the Denver and Rio Grande Narrow Gauge from Colorado Springs with the Denver Pacific out of Pueblo, stage traffic through central Colorado would cease to exist. Joe would continue to run the station for the Denver to Trinidad route, but its future use as a stage station was limited. Tisdale had found positions for part of the drivers and shotgun messengers, and a few of the station managers, but the rest would have to find other employment.

For Joe, Hannah and their coachmen, it was a heavy blow. Tisdale was on his way to Mozier to arrange the closing down of the station and the one east of it, called Landers Station.

Charles Youngblood would be offered another station in Wyoming, and his animal handler discharged after the sale of the property. Grover was being sent north to service a short, local run in isolated villages in Utah, which connected with the railroad. Rusty would be allowed to retire with a small pension because of his long service.

Tex Torrance and Mel, his guard, would be transferred to a route near Taos, in New Mexico Territory. Jim Owens would continue to drive up from the south, but a new guard would arrive in the next week. Fizzure Rodriguez resigned and headed for Texas when he received the news by telegram that the stage stations were being abandoned.

As for Joe and Hannah, he had the foresight to purchase the land and buildings; so the family would remain at Sweetwater Springs. As though in one of his nightmares, Joe looked about him at the buildings, sheds, and corrals he had built with his own hands, at the towering pine forest, the far distant mountains, and for the first time since coming home from the war, he felt depressed and angry. He saddled Mack and rode to the river boundary of his land. There he stood on the bank and let out a long, loud string of curses that would have made Rusty cringe in embarrassment. He cursed at the injustice, for his friends, for his lifestyle, and for the passing of an era. He cast his mind back to the first day, when he sat in the office of John Dempsey and was told of the position in Colorado at the base of the mountains. He thought of Matthew Baldwin just starting his career as a stage driver. He thought of Ned Baldwin and his wife and children. Of Taylor and Jackson and the building crew, of Buck Jones and Rosie, his Indian wife, and of Jeremiah Fuller, the Confederate soldier from Tennessee. The memories almost overwhelmed him as he dropped to the ground and sat hunched over and gazed at the fast-moving stream.

When he returned to the station, he was his calm, cheerful, charming self. He put the stallion away after a good rubdown and an extra portion of grain. He treated the guests, including Wallace Tisdale, with respect and dignity, but his heart was torn asunder. He and Hannah talked long into the night, while cozy and warm in their bed.

The next day, Ivan and Hank drove to the Mozier station with Tisdale on board. Hannah waved good-bye, but Ruth stayed in the kitchen with Fuller. One week later, on a Thursday, Rusty and Grover made the trip for the last time, carrying Tisdale and seven passengers on their way to Denver. The passengers included a disgruntled Charles Youngblood, his wife, Irma, and their two children. Also included were Art Finnegan, the former manager of Landers Station, and his wife, Zara. The Landers animal handler rode on horseback, and remained aloof from the other people. Enoch Barclay, the Mozier animal handler, visited in the barn with Roland and Ivan before stepping aboard the familiar brown coach, driven by Grover, with Rusty on the high seat serving as guard. His eyes remained focused straight ahead, and the old brown stage disappeared through the stately Ponderosas and the junipers and the spruce trees. There was no final loud, melodious sound of the trumpet to mark their passing.

They were followed by a line of three wagons full of supplies and furniture, and the three outriders hired by Tisdale, pushing the herd of mules and horses. Joe had selected four horses, including Modred, and the two yearlings, to be used by the stage line. He separated twelve mules to travel with them, since he would have no use for the stage mules used on the Mozier route. He kept the rest of the mules for his own use and paid Tisdale the stated price, without haggling. Some of the supplies, the goats and crates of chickens were left with Joe for the use of the station, and the rest would be offered to the manager at Buckboard Station. He watched until they were out of sight. The silence of the forest closed behind them, and the residents went about their work.

That evening, on schedule, Jim Owens and his new guard, Jude Quennell, drove into the yard with three ladies, two children, and two men. They were greeted by a circle of smiling faces, given a large meal and clean beds. While the horses were being hitched, the men discussed the events of the morning. Joe and Roland made their regular check of the vehicle and the animals. Jude sat grim and silent on the high seat with his shotgun across his lap, and Jim climbed into the box. His last words echoed around the station and mingled with the sound of children's laughter, a dog's barking and the creaking of harnesses and pounding hooves on the dusty ground as the coach rumbled across the creek and out of sight.

"See ya, next week, Joe."